A Candlelight Ecstasy Classic Romance

"WHY, ERIC?"

"Why what, little one?"

"Why did you leave so suddenly last night? H-how could you k-kiss me like that one minute and then just walk away? And to ask Maude and Bill to say good-bye for you, to have someone else tell me that we're never to see each other again? Why couldn't you tell me yourself? I-I never saw you as a coward—as flinching from the task of breaking it off with a woman—not from our first meeting! So why?"

"Look, Nicki, it would never work between you and me, we both know that. First of all, I'm not about to get married. I don't want to make any commitments to a woman. I can't give you what you want, honey. I'd only hurt you!"

CANDLELIGHT ECSTASY CLASSIC ROMANCES

CANDLELIGHT ECSTASY ROMANCES®

QUANTITY SALES

INDIVIDUAL SALES

THE
TEMPESTUOUS
LOVERS

Suzanne Simmons

A CANDLELIGHT ECSTASY CLASSIC ROMANCE

Published by
Dell Publishing Co., Inc.
1 Dag Hammarskjold Plaza
New York, New York 10017

Dell ® TM 681510, Dell Publishing Co., Inc.

A Candlelight Ecstasy Classic Romance

Candlelight Ecstasy Romance®, 1,203,540, is a registered trademark of Dell Publishing Co., Inc.

ISBN: 0-440-18551-3

Printed in the United States of America

One Previous Edition

April 1987

10 9 8 7 6 5 4 3 2 1

WFH

To Our Readers:

By popular demand we are happy to announce that we will be bringing you two Candlelight Ecstasy Classic Romances every month.

In the upcoming months your favorite authors and their earlier best-selling Candlelight Ecstasy Romances® will be available once again.

As always, we will continue to present the distinctive sensuous love stories that you have come to expect only from Ecstasy and also the very finest work from new authors of contemporary romantic fiction.

Your suggestions and comments are always welcome. Please write to us at the address below.

Sincerely,

The Editors
Candlelight Romances
1 Dag Hammarskjold Plaza
New York, New York 10017

THE
TEMPESTUOUS
LOVERS

CHAPTER ONE

The young woman quietly slipped into the study and closed the door behind her. Uttering a sigh of relief, she kicked off her high-heeled silver sandals, letting her feet sink down into the soft plush carpeting. After a moment, she strolled across the room to a velvet-draped window seat and leaned her aching head against the sill. As the throbbing in her temples began to recede, she curled up on the cushioned seat, neatly tucking her bare feet beneath the folds of her long skirt.

A small, finely shaped hand swept the mass of golden hair back from her face. Large, dark-rimmed hazel eyes sparkled with excitement as she gazed at the scene before her. It was a night in early June, with a touch of dampness in the air. A thousand twinkling lights gave Manhattan a celestial appearance. From where the girl was sitting, she felt as if she were precariously perched atop the world. This was the young woman's first visit to the States. In fact, it was her first time abroad, and the special pulse of New York had already captured her imagination. There was so very much she wanted to see and so many things she wanted to do.

The past several days had a dreamlike quality about them for the young woman. Could it really have been just three days since Nicki had sipped tea and munched on home-baked biscuits, biscuits she had made herself, in her father's bungalow in a tiny hamlet outside Wolverhampton? At least that's how people usually described Cheswick, though in reality the village was some distance from Wolverhampton.

And now, here she sat in the wood-paneled study of a luxurious apartment on the seventeenth floor of a Fifth Avenue high rise staring out at the world's most famous skyline. Everything here was modern, air-conditioned, and expensive. The contrast between this world and her own was mind-boggling. Just as the differences between Nicki and her hosts were immediately obvious, at least to her. Nicki could still hear the residue of the noisy cocktail party as it clammered on in the next room—the catalyst for her flight to the relative quiet of her uncle Bill's study.

The slim, fair-haired girl uttered a second sigh as she thought of her uncle Bill and aunt Maude. They were dears, really, in their own way. But they moved in a sophisticated, moneyed set that was chicly international. And since the New York season was almost at an end, the social pace was frenzied. For soon they would depart in twos or threes for the yacht cruise to the islands or perhaps to the borrowed villa by a cool lake or azure-blue sea. New York would lie dormant over the hot humid summer —left to the poor who had no place else to go, the working middle class, and the hordes of tourists.

Nicki found it all slightly overwhelming. It was still incomprehensible to her that the sleek, coutured Maude and her own mother had been sisters. For whenever thoughts of her mother eased themselves into Nicki's mind it was the memory of the woolly jumpers she had preferred to wear or the scent of the rose water she had favored. Nicki's mother had been a true country woman, just as the girl wished she would be one day, herself.

By some standards it might seem that Nicki had led a rather sheltered, perhaps even backward, existence the past twenty years and five months. She had been the only child of two adoring parents and then of a doting father who had been left a widower in the prime of life. Nicki had lived all of her years in the same familiar well-loved house in Cheswick, where her father was the village doctor, the leading bridge player, and in recent years Cheswick's most eligible bachelor. Except for a few months at secretarial school when she was eighteen, Nicki had never left home. She worked part-time in her father's office as his receptionist and secretary three mornings a week.

Having led a protected life did not mean that the young woman was uneducated. True, Nicki had not chosen to attend the university; still she was widely read and had studied classical piano since the age of seven. The well-polished grand piano that filled the front room had been her mother's and was the most cherished of the girl's possessions.

A sad, wistful smile softened the girl's features as she thought of home. It was the one spot in all the world where she felt completely free to be herself. Just as she was completely at ease with Mark Winstead, the local solicitor she had been keeping company with for the past year since his return from London. There was, as yet, no formal announcement of an engagement, but everyone in Cheswick knew that Mark had been in love with her since she was fourteen. He had been waiting all these years for Nicki to grow up into the woman he could ask to be his wife.

And as Nicki was quite fond of him too, she assumed that one day soon she would become Mrs. Mark Winstead. While the thought did not send her pulses racing, she felt happy and content at the prospect.

Born and bred in the English countryside, Nicki and Mark had known each other all of their lives. Indeed, it had been her father who had brought Mark into this world one gray January dawn twenty-six years earlier. And Mark himself could still vaguely recall his first glimpse of the newborn Swithin baby when he had been a remarkably precocious five-year-old peeking over the lacy edge of her cradle.

They were two of a kind, Nicki and this comfortable brown-haired man of hers in tweeds. They were content with the things in life that no amount of money could buy or lack of money destroy. They understood each other completely—there were no secrets between them, no mysteries. They trusted and respected each other, they believed in the same values, they wanted the same things from life. And it would be a good life, too, thought Nicki.

A solitary tear wedged itself loose from the corner of her eye and slowly slid over the porcelain-white cheek to finally fall unheeded upon the silky material of her blouse. Perhaps it had been a mistake to let her father and Aunt Maude persuade her to spend the summer in the United States. But even Mark had urged her to take advantage of the opportunity. So here she sat on a beautiful summer evening, her head aching, feeling terribly alone and a little sorry for herself, shut away from the glittering party in the next room.

Uncle Bill and Aunt Maude's friends seemed so intellectual and witty as they urbanely debated the relevance of this play or the interpretation of that concerto at Lincoln Center, or some "marvelous" new artist on exhibit at the

12

Guggenheim; or perhaps they had discovered a new night spot or smart boutique. Nicki had found it all a little boring, but very disconcerting too. She knew this older, fashionable crowd must find her terribly naive and amusingly quaint with her old-fashioned ideas and morals. And she possessed far too much self-respect to care for the thought of being laughed at by anyone. Her entire stay in New York had so far consisted of one awkward social event after another. What in the world was she doing here, she thought despairingly.

Yet—there was no denying that special something that existed about New York. Nicki had a whole long list of places and things she wanted to see and do. She didn't much care if people thought she was acting like a tourist—she was a tourist! Nicki wanted to climb to the very top of the Statue of Liberty, take a guided tour through the United Nations, ride in a hansom cab through Central Park, munch hot chestnuts from a street vendor, and walk down Broadway to Times Square at night. This was likely to be Nicki's one chance to see New York and it did seem such a waste to spend her precious two weeks in an endless round of parties with her aunt and uncle!

For in just over a fortnight, she would be boarding yet another jet that would whisk her off to Boston and then on to Bangor, Maine, and eventually she would end up in Bar Harbor, a resort community off the Atlantic coastline. There she would spend most of her summer with a second cousin once removed. Clare Trumbull and her husband, Nash, ran an antique shop and gift shop and Nicki would be working partly for her room and board. She had never met either of these American relations, but her father had assured her that they were most eager for her company and help. Nicki hoped their letters had been sincere, since she would be staying with them for several months.

A summer in Maine—an even bigger sigh escaped from Nicki's colorless lips at the prospect of what she had let herself in for.

"It would have been so much simpler for everyone if I'd just stayed at home," she groaned out loud, not knowing how the truth of those words would return to haunt her later.

Just for an instant, unable to separate dream from reality, Nicki believed herself to be back in her own room in England. Then came the realization, somewhat sadly, that she must have dozed off for a few minutes, for she was still curled up in the window seat in her uncle Bill's study. She had felt rather weary earlier that day and had rested in her room at the surprisingly maternal insistence of her aunt. And she knew from her father's instructions that it might be several days before the side effects of her trip wore off. Nicki yawned lazily and was about to straighten up and smooth away the creases from her skirt before rejoining the party, when the rich timbre of a masculine voice very close by stopped her cold.

"Nadine"—the voice cut through the silence of the room like a sharp knife—"we've been through all of this before. Dammit, woman, you know how I hate to be telephoned when I'm at a party! As soon as any woman starts checking up on me, she's written her own walking papers as far as I'm concerned," he said in a cold, uncompromising tone. "Professions of love from you, my dear. Don't disillusion me now. We're two of a kind, you said it yourself. You don't believe in love any more than I do. Let's at least say we were always honest with each other," the man suggested with ill-concealed sarcasm.

The voice was deep and resonant, forceful, sure, like that of an accomplished actor, analyzed Nicki. And there

14

was an undercurrent of cruelty and hardness, as well. She was tempted to risk a quick peek around the fringed edge of the drape to verify the image in her mind of this devil of a man, but her nerve failed her at the last moment and she silently sunk back even farther into the camouflage provided by the window seat. Should she let this intruder know he wasn't alone? The thought occurred to her suddenly. Or would it be better if she simply waited—waited for him to end his conversation and leave the room, never the wiser to her presence?

"You seem like an intelligent person, Nadine, surely I don't have to spell it out for a woman of your experience . . . very well, then, it's over and done with! There is nothing left between us. I don't know how to make it any clearer than that," he said in a tightly controlled voice.

All right, all right, thought Nicki as she squirmed uncomfortably. It's over between you and this woman. She must surely understand by now—even I understand, and I've never been known to be quick about these things. So hang up the receiver and leave, please, because I'm getting a ghastly cramp in my leg!

"I'm losing what little patience I have left, woman. Don't push me or I'll be forced to say things you'll regret! Your jealousy is consuming you, Nadine, can't you see that? It's turned you into an ugly, hysterical shrew. . . . There is no one else, not yet anyway. I just don't happen to want you anymore. It's as simple as that." The man paused momentarily, then continued in a tone totally devoid of mercy.

"I realize that a once-beautiful woman like yourself expects to be the one to end a liaison, Nadine. Just as you have done so many times before. . . . I am all too aware that I was not the first man in your life or the only one. But I'm not one of the simpering spineless idiots you usually take up with—I picked you up, remember, and now that it no longer amuses me, I am dropping you. You bore me insufferably, Nadine!"

"Oh, dear God," whispered Nicki miserably. Surely this devilish man was humiliating Nadine, whoever or whatever she was, more than any human being deserved. Had he no pity or mercy to show the woman? Nicki was quite certain about one thing—she did not like this man one bit and she prayed fervently that they need never meet. The young woman winced soundlessly as the pain in her calf increased, bringing her thoughts jolting back to her own precarious position. She was going to have to move—and soon, that's all there was to it!

For what seemed like hours, but was only a matter of a few minutes, Nicki heard only the bass rumblings of the music being played in the adjacent room. She finally decided that the intruder must be listening without comment to the woman on the other end of the connection. Several more long minutes passed by without a sound. Nicki was beginning to suspect that she was alone—that the man had somehow left the study when she had been preoccupied with her leg. He must have left and she simply had not heard him go. There was only one way to find out. She must risk a quick glance around the corner of the drape. Leaning forward she gathered some of the soft material in her trembling hand and pushed it back a fraction of an inch and looked out.

He was standing there—the receiver still clasped in his muscular, tanned hand, a puzzled expression on his dark features as he stared down at two silver shoes lying on the carpet in front of him. The very sandals Nicki had so casually kicked off her tired feet upon entering the room! An audible gasp escaped from the young woman before she could clamp her hand over her mouth. She was about to be found out!

Looking up she confronted two gray-blue eyes the color of the Northern Sea staring directly into her own. Every lean hard muscle of the man's body tensed—he was no less surprised than she had been at the discovery that he was not alone.

"W-what the devil . . . No, no, Nadine, I wasn't talking to you. I-I'm not alone, that's all. No, I've already told you, there is no other woman in my life. I just don't want you anymore." His statement was emphatic. A trace of boredom crept into his manner as he was forced to reiterate his disdain. The man's full attention had been diverted to the slim form crouched in the window seat. He motioned impatiently for whoever it was behind the large luminous eyes to come forth and reveal herself.

Nicki hesitated, her heart pounding wildly. She was trapped! There was no way she could escape this man now. Reluctantly she obeyed his unspoken command and proceeded from her hiding place. But not without a great deal of trepidation and misgiving on her part. For Nicki realized she had just overheard what had to be a most embarrassing conversation for this dark, scowling stranger. The young woman was just a little bit frightened by what his reaction to her might be. Trembling visibly, Nicki unfolded her slim legs and attempted to stand to face her accuser. But her legs gave beneath her and she fell back against the velvet backdrop. Stopping to massage her cramped muscle, she attempted to stand up for a second time.

"Huh—who's with me? No one you know, Nadine, so stop trying to be so clever. Yes, it's a girl. Listen, Nadine, I've had enough of your insinuations . . . I don't want to be deliberately cruel to you!"

Even from where she now stood, a good ten feet away,

Nicki heard the derisive laughter of the woman as it crackled over the line. Good Lord, thought the girl, Nadine was either half-mad or had consumed far too much alcohol. She sounded positively demonic. A shudder ran down Nicki's spine as the awful sound of the woman's crazed laughter came again and again. Nicki certainly didn't care to meet this woman as either a friend or an enemy.

Then the man spoke again, but his gaze never left Nicki's face, not even for a moment. He stared long and hard into her eyes before allowing his own appreciative eyes to take in each slender curve of her figure, outlined to perfection by the skirt she wore. The girl felt a telltale blush rise from her neck and spread to her pale cheeks as she watched the path of his scrutiny.

"All right, Nadine," he finally said in a weary, toneless voice. "I had hoped to spare you the agony, but if you must know then I'll confess everything. There is another woman. She is very young, very beautiful, and very innocent—three virtues you have sadly lacked for a long time. . . . No! You demanded to know all the bloody details—I wouldn't dream of disappointing you now. Let me tell you all about her," he snarled cruelly. "She's a lovely creature —long golden hair, skin as flawless as a piece of rare porcelain, large blue-green eyes, a young eager body on the brink of being awakened for the first time. She is, in fact, the very antithesis of yourself. That's what you wanted to hear, wasn't it? Well, now you have! . . .

"Yes, she's here, in the room with me now," he said quietly.

There was an audible string of oaths heard by them both before the man soundlessly replaced the telephone receiver. He had lit a small cheroot and was casually standing there smoking when the full significance of his words finally hit Nicki. Why, the unmitigated gall, the absolute

18

nerve of the man—he had described her to Nadine! And just how did he know so much about her, anyway?

Nicki's eyes opened even wider as she considered again what this infuriating man had implied to the woman on the telephone. Why, he had made it sound like they were about to become lovers! She stared dumbfounded at the stranger, unconsciously taking in the broad shoulders impeccably attired in what could only be a tailor-made dinner jacket, strong muscular legs set in a casual stance, expensive Italian shoes, hands resting on slim hips, penetrating blue eyes, black hair dusted with silver at the temples—all set off by a bronzed face that could only have been tanned that shade under a tropical sun.

"You like what you see." His voice cut into her thoughts abruptly, a statement of fact rather than a question.

Nicki shook herself fiercely. She had been gaping at this outrageously handsome man as if she were an adolescent schoolgirl or, worse yet, a country bumpkin. Well, she would show him that she was neither!

"W-well, of all the nerve!" she finally sputtered, wishing she could make her legs move, to somehow escape from this room. But she was incapable of taking even one step, as if she were glued to the very spot where she stood.

"I've never lacked for nerve in my entire life, child, not since I went out on my own at fourteen. You can't be gutless in business or pleasure—not if you want to succeed!" he teased expertly. "And you were staring at me, your mouth hanging wide open," he reminded her ungallantly.

"I-I was staring at you, s-sir," she stuttered furiously, gritting her teeth, "because I couldn't believe what you t-told that woman about me. Not because of your supposedly irresistible charms! You really are a conceited

19

man," she blurted out, "and I find your manner most offensive!"

"You find me offensive!" he exploded. "And what the hell makes you think I was describing you to Nadine?" He ground out his cigar in the ashtray at his elbow and took a menacing step toward the young woman.

"No! Don't back away!" he barked at her. "I repeat— what makes you think you were the young, innocent, beautiful creature whose virtues I extolled to my ex-. . . paramour?" He dragged out each word as if it were an insult.

The girl lowered her head self-consciously, unable to meet the dangerous challenge issued by the man's dark eyes.

"Well?" he demanded.

"I-I have blond hair," she began tentatively, "and m-my eyes are hazel . . . oh, go away!" cried Nicki in embarrassed confusion. "I-I don't want to talk to you anymore."

Ignoring her last statement as if it had never been uttered, the tall powerful stranger spoke again, but this time without the slightest hint of anger in his voice. "You know you really are a pretty little thing," he murmured.

"Please leave me alone," whispered Nicki ineffectually as a hot flush struck her face again.

"Don't you like receiving compliments?" he asked her, watching expectantly as she shook her head no, her golden hair shimmering in the lamplight. "You are a strange young thing then. I have found it is woman's nature to crave being reassured by the male of the species that she's attractive and desirable."

"Not me!" denied Nicki vehemently, snapping her head up, eyes flashing green and then blue, and finally almost a shade of yellow.

20

"But then you're not a woman really, are you?" mused the man out loud. "You're just a slip of a girl in a woman's body. Barely more than a child."

"I'll have you know, Mr. whoever-you-are, that I'm almost twenty-one years old!" She glared up at the man as he stood towering over her own five feet three inches by nearly a foot. "That's hardly a child in anyone's eyes, even to a 'mature' man like yourself."

"That old!" he said in a mocking tone. Nicki realized too late that he was simply baiting her and she had fallen for it.

"I think you're deliberately teasing me," she said, boldly looking up into his face. "And I always feel uncomfortable when a man who is old enough to know better tries to play games with me."

The handsome man put back his dark head and laughed full and out loud.

"I'm not certain, but I think the mouse just roared back at the lion," he chuckled. "My dear girl, you wouldn't know the first thing about the kind of games I play!" he stated in a condescending tone.

"How would you know?" she protested with a slight pout, a challenge unknowingly issued by her young lips.

"Oh, child," he warned in a low voice, "you'd better be careful when you extend such an obvious invitation to a man like me."

"I-I'm sure I don't know what you're talking about, Mr.
. . ."

"Eric Damon," he supplied.

"Mr. Damon."

"Eric."

"Mr. Damon," emphasized Nicki.

"And you are either the most naive young woman that I have ever met or else a rare and consummate actress," he suggested with a churlish grin upon his full sensuous mouth.

"And I can assure you, Mr. Damon," declared Nicki hotly, "that I am not an actress nor am I the childish creature you imply."

"Then that only leaves me to conclude that you have led a very dull existence . . . at least until now," he stated dryly.

"And it's obvious from your telephone conversation that your life is anything but dull. Well, if that's what you call exciting then you are more than welcome to it!" she retaliated.

"Do you always eavesdrop on other people's private affairs?" he pursued, the humor suddenly fading from his steel-blue eyes. "Is that how a girl like you gets her thrills? Playing it safe, living vicariously through someone else's love affair? Never getting involved yourself, safeguarding your precious virginity behind that cold blond beauty until some poor miserable slob comes along and puts a ring on your finger."

"What a terrible thing to say!" interrupted Nicki, her voice strangely hoarse. "You don't know anything about me, Mr. Damon. And I wasn't eavesdropping! I fell asleep and when I woke up you were already talking to th-that woman. I foolishly thought I could spare both of us a great deal of embarrassment," she explained louder than necessary. "Some things are simply not said in polite company, Mr. Damon. But then, perhaps that kind of sensitivity, that kind of good manners, would require the breeding of a gentleman!" Her implication was not lost on the tall stranger beside her.

"And I'm no gentleman, is that it? Ho—that's no insult, girl. I've known all along that I wouldn't want to be the kind of man you're talking about. I just wonder if you're

22

quite the lady you think you are. It might be amusing to find out." He muttered the last sentence under his breath. "And by the way, I'm not in the least embarrassed by the intimate conversation you overheard," he corrected her.

"Well, you should—" Nicki stopped in midsentence. The man's morals were not her concern, she reminded herself.

"What were you going to say?" pressured Eric as he studied the red blush rising to the tips of her small perfectly shaped ears.

"Nothing!"

"Liar! You know you were about to lecture me on my dubious behavior, my moral obligations, you were about to tell me that I should have been blushing with embarrassment at what you overheard," he supplied smugly.

"If you know so damn much, why ask me?" she demanded irritably.

"Perhaps because you turn the loveliest shade of pink and it's been a long time since I've met a gir—a woman who still had anything to blush about." He smiled gently, quite unexpectedly.

The sudden change in his attitude stumped the young woman. She found herself smiling back at the handsome man effortlessly.

"It's a terrible nuisance sometimes," she confessed shyly. "I can't even tell a little white lie without giving myself away."

"I can believe that," he laughed softly. "I bet you light up like a Christmas tree."

"You're so right," sighed the young girl as she unceremoniously plopped herself down on an empty corner of the massive mahogany desk.

"You have me at a distinct disadvantage, young lady!" he growled close to her ear.

23

"W-wh . . ." Nicki's eyes flew open.

"You know who I am, but I don't have the slightest notion who you are."

"Mr. Damon, you scared me!" she gasped, clutching her hand against her breast.

"Hey, I'm sorry, honestly," he apologized, a ridiculously contrite expression surfacing on his dark devilish features. All of a sudden, Nicki could visualize the young boy that Eric Damon may have once been, the mischievous child who no doubt had this same contrite expression on his face whenever he was caught with his hand in the cookie jar just before dinner.

The young woman's smile grew and then broadened until she started to laugh out loud, helpless to prevent the tears of mirth from streaming down her face. When she finally regained some measure of composure, she tried to give an explanation to the obviously puzzled man at her side.

"I-I'm sorry," she gulped, "but if you could have only seen your face."

"I'm glad I at least afford you some amusement," he said dryly, the arrogance stealing back into his manner.

"I'm sorry, Eric, really I am. But you were funny," she continued with a spasm of laughter.

"I have been called many things by many women, but never funny," he interjected. "And since you're calling me Eric now, might I not at least know your name, Miss . . ."

"Oh, I am sorry. It's Swithin, Nicole Swithin, but everybody at home calls me Nicki, Mr. Damon."

"Please, I want you to call me Eric," he reassured her as he stepped back behind the desk and eased himself into a swivel chair with the grace of a natural athlete.

"I-I don't usually presume to call a total stranger by their Christian name, sir. Especially one of my elders."

"Good Lord, I suddenly feel an attack of senility coming on!" he replied sarcastically.

"Oh—I didn't mean it that way!" Nicki pleaded with real penance in her voice. "Honestly, I don't think you're very old at all."

"I'm thirty-six, Nicki, or at least I will be in ten days. Almost old enough to be your father if I'd been precocious, and I was." The devilish glint returned to his eyes. "And we could hardly pretend that you and I are total strangers, now could we? Consider the circumstances of our meeting. Hardly the conditions under which a man normally makes the acquaintance of a young lady. You did hear a rather intimate exchange between myself and my former . . . now, what would be a delicate way of putting it for the ears of one so innocent—paramour? lover? bed partner?" Eric's face tightened as he taunted the girl; she became more pale with each word he spit out venomously at her.

"You're deliberately being vulgar," acknowledged Nicki unhappily. "Well, I'm not quite so easily shocked as you might think, Mr. Damon. My father is a doctor and I have seen some of the darker side of man's nature. But I would like to try and forget the circumstances of this meeting, that's for sure." The young woman unconsciously bit into her lower lip to prevent the tears from flowing. She had never met a man like Eric Damon before—never in her entire life!

"I don't suppose you've ever met someone like me before, have you, sweet young Nicki?" he half-growled as if he read her mind. "I can see censure in the tilt of your determined little chin and disapproval, perhaps even fright in your big hazel eyes. You don't approve of me, do

25

you, proper young English miss? For I have dared to offend your well-bred sensibilities. What cold fish you English are!" He twisted the words meaningfully as he spoke, lacing them with undisguised distaste.

"You seem very fond of labeling people without really knowing them," cried Nicki. "And anyway it's simply not true! The English are just more reserved than people here in the States. It's not a matter of who's right and who's wrong. It's the difference between cultures. Why, there's no more kind, warm-hearted souls anywhere on the face of this earth than the people in Cheswick. And villages like ours are scattered here and there all over England. You're wrong, Mr. Damon. The English are not cold fish!" she declared staunchly.

The man stared in amazement at the flushed, indignant face of the petite girl taking her stand before him like a defending knight of old.

"I feel like I've stumbled onto a hornet's nest," he mumbled incredulously. "Are you always so—so emotional, so quick to jump to the defense?"

"Of course, if it's something I really believe in or feel strongly about," said Nicki. "Don't you?"

"An idealist yet," he muttered unintelligibly.

"Did you say something, Mr. Damon?" the girl inquired with wide-eyed innocence.

"I-I was just wondering where this village, this paragon of humanity called Cheswick, is located," he remarked. "No doubt in the very heart of England herself!"

"You may mock us, but the people in our village really care about each other," she replied quietly. "We're like a family, though it's nicer than most because we choose to be together. Haven't you ever been lonely?"

He answered with complete candor, unprepared for her question as he was.

26

"Haven't we all been?" His eyes softened for a moment —perhaps even a flicker of pain was to be seen there if Nicki had looked up.

"No one ever need be lonely in Cheswick. There is always someone who will understand, someone to be there when you need them, to lend a warm hand to hold on to when you feel the need to touch another human being. To reassure yourself it will be all right, no matter how insurmountable the problem may seem. Cheswick is a lovely place, Eric. I'd never live anywhere else." Nicki smiled bemusedly as she let her mind wander, recalling the patch of wildflowers she and Mark had discovered by the old stone bridge just the day before she had left home for London. She was suddenly terribly homesick. Why was she here in New York, stuck at a noisy party with a hard, unkind stranger when she could be at home with Mark and her father, neither of whom had ever even raised his voice to her?

The girl was completely ignorant of the breathless picture she presented as she sat perfectly still—like some wild creature poised for flight but as yet unaware of its human observer. It was some seconds before Eric Damon could bring himself to intrude upon her musings.

"It sounds like a regular Brigadoon," he speculated, his voice harsher than he meant it to be.

"I suppose I have made it sound a bit idyllic." The hurt she felt at his unspoken criticism was all too evident in her tone. "I mean we do have our problems too. But Cheswick is a very nice place," the girl said earnestly. "I don't suppose it's changed much since the war."

"Since the war," repeated Eric incredulously, studying the young woman's face as if he half-expected her to be joking. "Since the war! I'm almost afraid to ask which war, Nicki. Wake up, girl! You're living in a dream world

27

that doesn't exist anymore, if in fact it ever did! This is the twentieth century, Nicki." He rose out of his chair as if he were somehow angry with the slender blond girl perched on the edge of the desk. Eric paced back and forth in front of Nicki, a fire ignited within him by her innocent remark.

"Nice! Nice is such a proper, genteel, middle-class description pompous people pin on mediocrity. I have found 'nice' places and 'nice' things and 'nice' people are at their best boring. At their worst they can destroy other people with their niceness!" He glared viciously at Nicki, but somehow she knew he wasn't seeing her at all. Seizing her slim shoulders he shook her until her very teeth rattled.

"Eric—Eric, y-you're hurting me," she whimpered as the man's fingers unknowingly bruised her flesh. She gazed at him in bewilderment, his lean dark features grown black with almost uncontrollable rage.

"You're hurting me," she repeated in a stronger voice.

"W-what? What did you say?" Eric asked after a moment, passing a trembling hand over his eyes.

"I said you're hurting me, Eric."

"Oh, God, Nicki, I'm sorry," he said in a nearly normal tone of voice. "Have I hurt you badly? Let me see," and without further thought he began to push the silky blouse from her shoulder.

"Please! It's all right!" Nicki cried out. "Please, don't touch me!"

Eric drew back sharply, the icy veneer returning to his face.

"I-I don't like to be touched by strangers, that's all," rationalized Nicki out loud. "A-and besides, you startled me."

"You're lying—your face is as red as a beet," he said, exasperated. "Admit it—you don't know what it's like to be touched by a man and you're afraid to find out."

"Perhaps I am, perhaps I think I have good reason to be," added Nicki as she rubbed the bruised spot on her shoulder. "You're a strange, violent man, Eric Damon," she continued thoughtfully. "One moment you seem almost kind, the next you're in a blind rage. I don't understand you one bit!"

"And you think a young, inexperienced slip of a kid like you can analyze a man almost twice your age and certainly twice your experience!" He laughed mirthlessly, his eyes unreadable, his forehead wrinkled in a frown. "I think it's time I sent you home to Mama, baby."

"My mother is dead, Mr. Damon. But you're right about one thing. There has been nothing in my life to prepare me to deal with a cynical, cruel, and merciless man like yourself.

"I don't like you," she whispered in desperation. "I want you to leave me alone. I don't understand a man like you. I don't know what you want from me. A man like you is poison to someone like me, I feel it!" Nicki's voice was barely audible as she had buried her trembling chin in the collar of her blouse. She twisted her hands nervously, afraid to look up and see Eric's reaction to her statements.

"There is absolutely nothing a man like me could want from a girl like you," he said as if every word were an insult. "Except perhaps first chance to introduce those innocent lips to the passions of womanhood." The broad-shouldered man put one of his bronzed hands on each side of Nicki's face and drew her toward him.

"P-please, Eric . . ."

"Please, Eric, what, Nicki? Please, Eric, kiss me? Haven't you ever wondered what it would be like to be kissed by a man, a real man, by a man like me?"

"N-no," she denied breathlessly, shaking her head from side to side within his grasp, her eyes closed in fear.

"I must be out of my mind," he snorted. "You're just a child. Get out of here before I do something we'll both regret!" He stepped away from the young woman and turned his back to her trembling figure.

"Get out!" he spat fiercely. "Just get the hell out!"

Nicki sat motionless for a moment, stunned by his bitterness. Oh, how she could hate this man. Then she slid off the well-waxed mahogany desk and ran for the door, afraid to look back at the tall, brooding figure in the study.

CHAPTER TWO

It was late the next morning when a stream of bright sunlight filtering in through the gossamer-thin drapes finally awakened Nicki. She had tossed and turned fitfully until the gray dawn stealthily crept into the city, bringing blissful unconsciousness to her exhausted body and mind. The roar of the metropolis that natives found as soothing as a bedtime lullaby had created havoc in the country girl. In truth, that was only one factor causing Nicki's insomnia. The dark scowling face of the stranger she had encountered in the study and his hateful, scathing words went round and round in the girl's brain until her headache had reached migraine proportions.

She moved gingerly at first awakening, testing the effect of movement upon her head. The pain had receded to a small dull ache at the base of her neck. As she propped herself up on the soft pink pillows of the mammoth bed, a firm knock came at her door.

"Come in," she called out. Her aunt entered in a flurry of feathers and embroidered silk.

31

"Good morning, darling," Maude Benson bubbled cheerfully. "I hope you've slept well. Is that dreadful headache of yours gone?" The concern in her voice was genuine. She sat down on the far edge of the bed and peered at the young woman with nearsighted, myopic eyes. "I've forgotten to put my contact lenses in this morning, my dear, so you seem rather out-of-focus to me."

"I'm fine now, Aunt Maude," answered the girl truthfully. The night before took on the aspect of a nightmare that was forgotten upon awakening. "I suppose I drank a little too much champagne for my first time out," she lied sheepishly.

"Well, I'm glad you're feeling no ill effects this morning, Nicki. I don't bounce back quite so quickly anymore, myself," she said with a tired sigh, faint dark spots visible beneath her carefully made-up eyes.

"Why, Aunt Maude, you're the most glamorous woman I've ever seen," complimented her astonished niece.

"It takes a great deal of time and effort to maintain glamour, Nicki. Don't let anyone kid you otherwise. And I'm beginning to feel my age," she said a little sadly.

"But, you're so much younger than Mum was. You can't be more than thirty-five," exclaimed the girl.

"Thank you, child, I needed to hear that this morning. But I'm afraid I'm much nearer to forty-five. There was only a year between Abigail and me, although I'd always given the impression there was more. Perhaps I wouldn't mind growing older so much if I'd had a daughter like you, Nicki. Abigail always was the lucky one," ended her aunt wistfully, her long, perfectly manicured hands playing with the folds of her dressing gown.

"But enough 'wool-gathering,' my dear," Maude said with sudden effervescence. "I came to find you because I have some plans to discuss with you before luncheon."

"Lunch!" Nicki fumbled for her watch on the night table. "What time is it? Oh, my gosh, half-past twelve! It's positively sinful. I'd never be in bed at this hour at home—everyone would assume you were ill," she confessed with a grin.

"Well, this is New York, not Cheswick, and it's not at all unusal here, so don't feel too sinful." The older woman chuckled at the contrite expression on her niece's unlined face. She really did have lovely skin, thought Maude. And Nicki was such a sweet child, rather like dear Abigail.

"Now, Nicki," began Maude in her smooth sophisticated tones, "there is no need for Bill and I to have to be told that our social affairs have been a bit boring for a young thing like you. No, don't deny it, darling. One of your greatest charms is that you are totally transparent," she said dryly. "And I know, too, that you're eager to do some sightseeing. So I have arranged for a friend of ours to show you around New York. Your uncle and I have full calendars or else we would take you ourselves. But as I've said I have just the person to show you the city. So put on something attractive yet comfortable and I'll have Maria bring you your tea. Eric will be here in half an hour. I believe he mentioned something about starting with luncheon in Central Park," explained Maude loquaciously.

"Eric?" Nicki's voice came out as a squeak. It couldn't be, she thought to herself, it just couldn't be. The name must be pure coincidence.

"Yes, dear, the man's name is Eric Damon. And he'll be here in a few minutes so you'd better get a move on it," urged her aunt as she nudged Nicki toward the shower and handed her a towel. "Your tea will be waiting, darling." And then Maude Benson was gone through the door without giving her niece even the slightest chance to speak.

Left standing there with a towel clutched in her hands, Nicki was dumbfounded by the latest turn of events. Well, she'd just get dressed and march right out and tell Eric Damon what he could do with his invitation! Pleased with her solution, she turned on the shower and let the steaming hot water beat down on her half-awake body.

Some minutes later a discreet, well-rehearsed rap at the door of the bedroom interrupted Nicki's harried thoughts. She had been going over in her mind exactly what she planned to say to Mr. Eric Damon. The small dark figure of the Bensons' maid appeared silently.

"Mr. Damon is here, Miss Swithin," she announced.

"All right, Maria, thank you. . . . Damn!" exclaimed the girl out of frustration as her trembling fingers fumbled with the elusive buttons of her sundress.

"Would you like me to help you with that, miss?" offered Maria in her softly accented voice.

"Oh, would you?" cried Nicki with genuine relief. "I-I seem to be so frightfully nervous, Maria."

"Mr. Damon is different from your usual sort of escort, *sí?*"said the small woman as she buttoned the girl's dress.

"*Sí!* Mr. Damon is very different from my usual dates!" laughed Nicki nervously. "Does he come here often? Is he a good friend of my aunt and uncle's?"

"No, he—he is a man apart, little one, not really close friends with anyone. But when he is in New York he always gives a small, but exquisite dinner party for Señor and Señora Benson. And I believe he counsels your uncle in his business as well. Ay—now I have talked too much and your aunt will begin to wonder where I have disappeared to. You look very lovely, miss. That shade of green is just right for your eyes," added Maria with an encouraging smile. "Shall I tell Mr. Damon and Señora Benson that you will be joining them in a moment?"

"Yes, please do, Maria, and thank you, again," said Nicki warmly.

"Why am I so nervous? He's just a man!" repeated Nicki out loud to herself when she was alone again, wishing that somehow the butterflies in her stomach would go away. "Because he's the most attractive man you've ever met and the most dangerous," she admitted to the four walls of the pink satin room. Squaring her slim shoulders, she studied herself in the full-length mirror that covered the closet door.

Maria was right, that shade of green did highlight her eyes to perfection, framed by the natural wave of her blond hair. And the rich leathery look of her shoes and handbag were a tasteful accompaniment. The short hem of her skirt made her slim legs appear even longer than they were. She was reasonably pleased with the girl in the mirror.

Jutting out her small dimpled chin, she assumed a mask of false courage much as a youth going into battle for the first time must do to prevent himself from turning tail and running in the opposite direction. Then she stepped out to meet Eric Damon.

"Ah, here she is now, Eric," acknowledged Maude Benson as Nicki crossed the expanse of the large living room toward them. "You look very nice, my dear," said her aunt in a satisfied tone. "Eric, I would like to introduce my . . ."

"Hello, Nicki," he interrupted Maude unceremoniously.

"H-hello, Mr. Damon," mumbled the girl stiffly as she stared at the wiry dark hairs of his chest that were revealed by the open blue silk shirt he wore. He was dressed in a fawn-colored suit, his shirt the exact same shade as his

35

eyes, as he knew only too well, Nicki thought. Drat, the man was good-looking!

"I thought we'd settled all that last night," he said in a soft, caressing tone.

"I suppose so," she responded unhappily.

"Well—then it's 'Hello, Eric,' " he prompted.

"All right. Hello, Eric," she repeated, finally looking up at him.

"Have you two met?" queried Maude with a funny look on her face as she watched the exchange between the tall dark man and her young niece.

"Yes, just briefly in Bill's study during last night's noisy bash," he expounded with a devilish gleam in his eyes. "I believe I disturbed a little nap Nicki was taking. Your niece elucidated several points for me, Maude. I found her candor most refreshing."

"Then you must surely realize that the idea of us having lunch together and spending the afternoon sightseeing is ludicrous!" offered Nicki. "We didn't really hit it off too well, Maude, if you want to know the truth," she added for her aunt's benefit.

"Nonsense, girl, just because you overheard my telephone conversation and I caught you at it and embarrassed you is no reason to deny me the pleasure of your company now."

"I wish someone would please tell me what you're talking about," interjected Maude Benson.

Before Eric Damon could explain more fully, Nicki cut in sharply. "Look, if we're going out to lunch, don't you think we should be going?"

"As a matter of fact, we must be off. I made reservations for half past one," he told her aunt calmly, ignoring the daggers Nicki's eyes were shooting in his direction.

"Have a nice afternoon, you two," called Maude as an

afterthought. But the large carved double doors to the apartment had already closed behind the man and the girl at his side.

Neither spoke until they were comfortably settled in the steel-gray Mercedes parked in front of the fashionable address.

"Mr. Damon . . ." began the girl.

"Look, Nicki, do me a favor," insisted the dark man gently. "Call me Eric. It will make our afternoon together more enjoyable for both of us. Let's make the best of . . ."

". . . of a bad situation neither of us wanted," she finished for him.

"If you say so," he answered a little gruffly as he swung the automobile into the busy traffic with graceful expertise.

"Aren't you curious about where I'm taking you?" Eric finally asked her.

"Maude said something about lunch at Central Park," muttered the girl unenthusiastically.

He swung toward her angrily as the car idled at a stoplight. "Well, for God's sakes, girl, can't you muster a little more enthusiasm than that? We're stuck with each other for the next five hours so let's make the best of it!"

She looked at him, startled and wide-eyed, and a little afraid. "All right, Eric. I'm sorry," she apologized.

"That's better. I thought we'd start with lunch at the Tavern-on-the-Green, followed by a stroll through the formal conservatory gardens. Then we'll go on to the United Nations and wind up the afternoon by stopping to see a special friend of mine," he outlined. "Do my plans meet with your approval, Miss Swithin?" he asked dryly.

"W-why, of course. I didn't mean to be so contrary. It's

really very nice of you to take me around. Oh—I'm sorry Maude imposed upon you, Eric," Nicki blurted out.

"So, that's what's been bothering you!" he said with a relieved laugh. "You silly child, I volunteered for this tour of duty."

Nicki sat perfectly still, stunned by his confession, staring at the enigmatic profile of the man beside her.

"Volunteered!"

He laughed. "I wanted to show you that I'm not always rude, bossy, and oversexed. To make up for the way I acted last night. I had had one martini too many and I wasn't in the best frame of mind after talking to Nadine."

"Oh," she said, a trifle disappointed somehow, and then she fell silent, unable to think of anything else to say to him.

"This is a very nice automobile," she said blandly after a time.

"Uh-huh."

"Do you live in New York?" she ventured forth again.

"Curious about me, Nicki?"

"Making polite conversation," she corrected him.

"If you say so. Actually, I have an apartment here mostly for business reasons. I keep a house in London, a flat in Rome, and a summer place in New England," he listed nonchalantly.

"Are you fabulously wealthy?"

"It's true—that I have a lot of money," he answered thoughtfully, almost as if he meant to say more and then changed his mind. He watched the girl's placid features out of the corner of his eye as he asked her a question of his own.

"Have you ever wished you had a lot of money, Nicki? To be able to buy whatever your heart desired?"

"I know this will sound terribly naive to you . . . but the

answer is 'no.' You see, money can't buy the things that really mean a lot to me, Eric." She was almost whispering.

"And what is your heart's desire, Nicole Swithin?" He had stopped the sleek gray auto and slid his arm along the back of the seat behind her. The warmth of his hand on the nape of her neck suddenly made clear thinking impossible for Nicki. She was very much aware of this tanned, lean man staring into her face as if he really wanted to know her answer.

"I-I want a husband who loves only me, a home of my own, happy children, good friends, my books, and my music," she said quietly.

"I believe you mean that," he said, his hard features momentarily softened. Then he bent forward and placed a gentle kiss on her pale lips. "You are a nice kid."

"Kid?" she picked up defensively.

"Hold on now, Nicki, don't get riled. We're there. You must be famished coming away without any breakfast and the food here is delicious," he said in a soothing tone.

Helping her from the car, Eric took her arm and guided her toward the gay, picturesque café on the green. Bright checkerboard cloths covered the round tables scattered here and there under big broad umbrellas.

"Ah, monsieur, we are pleased to see you again," greeted the maître d' as he rushed forth to meet Eric Damon and the fresh young girl at his side.

"Hello, Maurice. This is Miss Swithin, visiting us for a short while from England."

"Bonjour, mademoiselle." He bowed with a slight inclination of his bald head. *"Elle est très belle,"* he said aside to the man. "May you enjoy your stay in our fair city," he added to Nicki.

"Thank you, *merci bien,"* murmured the girl prettily.

"Your usual table has been prepared for you, Mr. Damon," stated Maurice as he led them toward a large yellow umbrella.

"We'll begin with escargot, Maurice. Do you have fresh crab today?"

"For you, most assuredly," answered the short stocky maître d'.

"I'll have a dry martini, the young lady will have fruit juice." Eric Damon concluded his business and transferred his attention to the young woman seated at his right.

"And what if I don't like crab, Mr. Eric Damon," she spat out as soon as they were alone. "Are you always so bossy or is it just with me?"

"You will learn, child, that a gracious woman allows her escort to choose for her, especially when he is familiar with the cuisine and she is not," he corrected her firmly. "Don't you like crab?"

"I love crab! That's not the point and you know it!" she answered testily. "I can speak for myself. I am not a child."

"Then don't persist in acting like one," he scolded her.

"Stop treating me like one," she said again. "You really are a frustrating man!" When it became apparent he was not going to respond, she went on. "Who's the friend you're taking me to see?"

"Madame Olivetti," he answered without further explanation. Before she could question him their drinks arrived and the conversation went into neutral territory.

Once she let herself relax, Nicki began to enjoy her outing with Eric Damon. In between bites of the most delectable morsels she had ever eaten, she chatted to him about her home in Cheswick, her father, and her few brief months at school in London, revealing more about herself to the man than she was cognizant of. Surprisingly, Eric Damon turned out to be an accomplished listener, asking just the right question at the right time and appearing to be truly interested in everything she told him. Nicki found she was enjoying herself immensely.

And to her further delight, she discovered her guide to be well versed on many of the varieties of flora at the formal gardens. It seemed an odd thing for a man like Eric to be interested in, she thought.

Then Nicki found herself standing outside a wafer-thin skyscraper—a structure of blue glass and hard steel rising from the edge of the East River—the United Nations, the commune of nations with its colorful display of each member's national banner fluttering in the brisk wind.

"May we go inside? Can we take one of the guided tours?" she queried eagerly.

"Your wish is about to come true," smiled Eric as they made their way through a small crowd of brightly clad visitors at the entrance.

Two hours later they emerged into the late afternoon sun.

"My head is spinning with the myriad of information that has just been crammed into it," she confessed to her companion. "And my feet are killing me!" she smiled at him. "But I've had a wonderful afternoon, Eric. This is the way I wanted to see New York."

"The best is yet to come, in my opinion," he told her. "We'll walk from here if you don't mind . . . just to Forty-second Street. Madame Olivetti lives there, in Woodstock Towers." He pointed ahead of them to an older structure standing diagonally across from the United Nations building.

"Who is Madame Olivetti, Eric?" Her interest was aroused.

"She is a marvelous living example of where determination and belief in oneself will get you. She came to New York forty years ago from an Iowa farm with only a few dollars in her pocket and her God-given talent. She worked her way through the Juilliard School of Music on a scholarship and eventually went on the concert tour. Then times got hard and she came back to New York permanently and became a private tutor. Madame Olivetti has lived by herself in the same one-room apartment for thirty years, Nicki. She never married, nor had the normal life that most women have, and yet she is fulfilled—she has seen the world through an artist's eye," Eric stated with something akin to reverence in his voice. "She still occasionally plays at the insistence of a close friend if her hands aren't too stiff that day. For the past five years she has suffered from rheumatoid arthritis."

"Why, she's a pianist, isn't she?" exclaimed the young woman. "How did you know I would be interested, that I play myself?"

"I have my ways," he said with an inscrutable expression on his face.

They entered the antique elegance of a former time in the faded lobby of Woodstock Towers and took the slow-moving elevator to the eighth floor. There Eric directed her to the rose-colored door of apartment number 808.

He pressed the buzzer and spoke into the small gray intercom beside the doorbell.

"It's Eric, Madame Olivetti. I have brought my friend to meet you."

"Eric, how good it is to see you again," came the clear, bell-like voice of the ageless woman with the auburn hair and sharp gray eyes who appeared momentarily before them in the open doorway. "Come in, come in!"

42

"And this is Nicole Swithin," he announced as he signalled for Nicki to precede him.

"Hello, my dear," greeted the woman. "My, but you're a young thing. You mustn't mind me, child. One of the advantages of growing old is that one can be dreadfully rude and it is excused as eccentricity," she chuckled merrily. "You're just in time for sherry and cookies."

They entered the apartment and Nicki immediately liked what she saw. One entire corner of the pale blue room was taken up by a Steinway grand piano that shone dark and deep with years of loving care. A daybed with a plain rose coverlet occupied a second corner. Lace curtains covered dust-bespeckled windows where satin roses grew without the aid of sunlight. There were several small tables and chairs and an antique love seat in front of a painted Chinese desk to fill the remainder of the room.

"You may wash up through that door if you like," indicated Madame Olivetti to the girl. "I'll get the sherry and tin of cookies before we sit down for our chat," she said as she patted Eric's arm. "I must thank you again, dear boy, I have enjoyed the French chocolates more than you know." She opened the louvered doors at the far end of the room to reveal a compact kitchenette complete with apartment-size refrigerator, stove, and sink.

It was an enchanting room, thought Nicki, as she repeated this thought to her hostess.

"I love my home—I have been here for three decades," the woman said fondly. "Every square inch of this apartment is as well known to me as the back of my own hand."

Nicki excused herself and went to wash her hands and freshen her makeup—more to give Madame Olivetti a few minutes alone with her handsome visitor than from necessity. When Nicki noiselessly stepped back into the main room, she paused at the sight of Eric Damon and Madame

Olivetti sitting side by side, her wrinkled, rhuematic hand resting in his, small bright eyes gazing up into laughing blue ones as they talked quietly.

"Ah—here she is," said the small woman as she spied the young woman coming toward them. "Let's have our sherry now, shall we?"

Nicki was comfortably settled back in a large over-stuffed chair nibbling on a cookie between sips of her wine when Madame Olivetti turned to speak to her.

"Eric has been telling me that you are quite an accomplished pianist yourself, Miss Swithin. Perhaps later you will indulge an old woman and play for me. I am not able to play much myself these days, but I do enjoy hearing young talent."

"I-if you like, of course, I'll play for you, Madame."

Minutes later Nicki settled herself at the Steinway, wiping her damp palms on her skirt in an unconsciously nervous gesture. Then she lightly touched the opening chords of Debussy's "Clair de Lune" and her butterflies vanished as they always did once she started to play. With head slightly bent, her golden cap of hair catching the late afternoon sun as it streamed in through the windows, she lost herself completely in her music. Leaving her mood of reverie, she moved on to Gershwin's "An American in Paris" and then demonstrated her virtuosity with Rachmaninoff's Concerto Number Thirteen before ending with the hauntingly melodic love theme "An Affair to Remember."

As the last note faded away, the young woman sat without moving, head bowed in concentration, unaware of the other two occupants of the room at that moment. Then she raised her pale face and turned to look at Eric and Madame Olivetti, surprised to discern the strong emotions on both their faces brought about by her music.

"Bravo, Nicole, bravo," said the older woman in a whisper. "You are a fine musician as you no doubt know. Your technique is excellent, but you also possess that rare and elusive gift—the ability to make your music come alive for those who are fortunate enough to hear it. I think in another year, with the proper guidance, you would be ready to begin the concert tour—if the desire is there. It takes dedication and determination to succeed as a professional. I speak from personal experience—I know the sacrifices it requires of the artist. I wonder if you are strong enough for that kind of life, my child?" Madame Olivetti fell silent.

"You sound just like Gaby when you say that, Madame. She said very much the same thing to me last summer," murmured Nicki affectionately.

"Gaby? Gaby? Who is this Gaby?" asked Madame Olivetti, suddenly animated.

"Actually, it's my godmother—Gabriella Fontini," replied the girl.

"You are Gabriella's goddaughter!" repeated the auburn-tressed woman as she shook her head in wonder. "I should not have been surprised by your talent if I had known that. This may sound trite, but it is indeed a small world. My dear Nicole, Gabriella Fontini and I were students together in our youth. Oh, so many years ago now we both performed on the concert stage in Europe. She stayed on and became famous, while I returned to this country and became a teacher. We have not seen each other for thirty years and neither of us were particularly prolific as a correspondent. You must tell me all about her and yourself too. Friends of our youth can be a joy in later years—I will write to Gabriella. Yes, I will write her! But first, tell me how you came to know Gabriella Fontini!"

45

She leaned forward eagerly and urged the young woman to begin.

The neon brilliancy of the city was lit up in full array by the time Nicki and Eric Damon stepped out onto the street again.

"You have made Madame Olivetti very happy, little one. It was a chance to relive some of the pleasant memories of her youth. Our visit was an even bigger success than I expected it to be," he said thoughtfully, as he took her by the arm and escorted her toward his car.

"She's an exceptional woman," replied the girl. "Who wouldn't be delighted and honored to meet someone like her. You were right, you know. Meeting your special friend was the very best part of a day filled with the best. I have truly enjoyed this day with you, Eric. I'll remember it for a long time," Nicki said a little breathlessly, as they scurried toward the gray Mercedes.

Seemingly preoccupied, Eric did not answer her. He removed his hand from her arm and reached to unlock the automobile. Then before she could slip into the subdued luxury of the car, he put both of his tanned hands on her shoulders and stared down into her youthful face softened by the hazy street light.

"Nicki." His voice had a strangely expectant tone about it. "Tomorrow morning we start with the Statue of Liberty, tomorrow night we'll promenade up Broadway."

"Oh . . ." was all the girl had a chance to say before his warm mouth descended upon hers for a brief instant. Then he was packing her into the car.

"Come on, it's definitely time for me to take you home," he said with a grin. "Or else I'll forget all my noble intentions."

Nicki managed a nod, but when Eric's full attention

seemed to be on making his way through the traffic of Manhattan, she raised one finger to the lips still remembering his kiss. And she couldn't help but wonder what his caress would be like if he thought of her as a woman rather than a half-grown child.

The same thoughts were still racing through her mind when she finally crawled into the pink queen-sized bed that night. A quiver ran through her slim body at the prospect of submitting to a dark, passionate male like Eric Damon.

"Get a hold of yourself, Nicki," she muttered in the dark, laughing at herself for speaking out loud when there was no one else there. "Your imagination is definitely working overtime and you've always been such a sensible girl. The man is almost old enough to be your father—well, a young uncle, anyway. And you certainly are **not** his type, even if you were a little older. I can just see the sleek, sophisticated, beautifully dressed women that he's attracted to. You're not his type! And he's not your type either—remember that! Please remember that!" She turned over and strained to put the image of the handsome Eric Damon from her mind. But it was very late before she finally drifted off to sleep.

CHAPTER THREE

Nicki was humming absentmindedly as she sat at the pink satin dressing table carefully maneuvering a pair of sheer stockings onto her slender legs. This was followed by black lacy undergarments. Then she stepped across to the closet and stood contemplating its contents for a moment before taking out a floor-length black sheath slit up each side in the mandarin style, a deliciously sophisticated dress Nicki had purchased that afternoon under the slightly disapproving eye of Maude Benson. She had never owned a dress like this before. But this was New York, not Cheswick, she told herself. And even a levelheaded female like herself was not immune to the natural desire to look très chic.

It was a very special dress for a very special night, she thought. This was Eric's thirty-sixth birthday and the two of them were celebrating with dinner at "21," and then on to a string of nightspots where they would dance until the wee hours of the morning. Without having analyzed her motives in depth, Nicki simply knew that she wanted to look grown-up for this evening with Eric Damon.

The past ten days had been crammed with museum tours, sightseeing, restaurants, and theaters, as Eric squired her from the Tappan Zee to the Battery and beyond. They had cruised around the island of Manhattan on a three-hour scenic boat trip, climbed breathlessly to the top of the Statue of Liberty, and rode the elevator all 102 floors of the Empire State Building to peer down at the minuscule humans below. Walking arm-in-arm they explored the Romanesque chapel and rare pieces of medieval art housed in the Cloisters. They walked and walked and walked—the American Museum of Natural History, the Metropolitan Museum of Art, Hayden Planetarium—until Nicki, worn out and with blistered feet, was forced to pull off her sandals and carry them home.

They munched hotdogs and popcorn and gulped down colas at a boxing exhibition in Madison Square Garden, ate hot thick pretzels lavished with mustard on a deserted street corner in the middle of a rainy Sunday afternoon, and watched transfixed as a chef in the window of a Broadway pizzeria flung a circle of dough into the air with the grace and confidence of an artist, only to retrieve it in midair with bored nonchalance. Eric insisted it was all part of her American education.

He took her to see *La Bohème* at Lincoln Center and she discovered that he, too, preferred light opera and Bach to Wagner and Beethoven. Early one morning he had driven her north out of the city in his gray Mercedes to Tarrytown, New York, where they toured "Sunnyside," the quaint residence of the nineteenth-century author Washington Irving.

Nicki saw the high-kicking Rockettes, Chinatown, Jones Beach, the garment district, Wall Street, and the seemingly mass confusion of the stock exchange. It was at the latter that the young woman inadvertently found out that the confusion evidently made a great deal of sense to her escort. Eric had excused himself for a moment and crossed the room to speak to a distinguished-looking white-haired gentleman, when Nicki overheard several men in dark business suits discussing someone of importance.

"There he is," one man commented to the other.

"So that's the great financial wizard!" his companion replied. "Huh, he sure seems to have everything—youth, looks, tremendous wealth. Some men are born lucky, I guess!"

"Don't kid yourself, Damon has made his own luck. The guy is shrewd, but totally ruthless. He's got no heart, he doesn't ever let anyone or anything get in his way," the second man muttered bitterly as they walked away.

Nicki had stood frozen to the spot, her heart pounding loudly in her ears, every nerve ending atingle. The man's words rang in her ears: "He's got no heart . . ." Her heart had cried out in desperation that he had been kind and thoughtful and patient with her. It couldn't all be just an act, or could it? She wanted to believe in the Eric that she had come to know over the past week more than anything in the world. And at that moment she had looked up to see the dark head and the mesmerizing smile on Eric's face as he strolled back across the room to her side. She had instantly forgotten the conversation she had just overheard.

By the end of the week, Nicki felt as if she had seen and done all there was to see and do in New York, yet she realized this was far from the truth. It had been a glorious whirlwind, all the same. And throughout it all, Eric had assumed a hands-off attitude, mentally as well as physically. He had played to perfection the role of the kindly uncle showing his young charge one of the great cities of the world. Nicki could not criticize his behavior—it had been exemplary. Yet somehow it left the girl with an empty, hollow ache in the pit of her stomach when he bade her "Sleep well" each night with a perfunctory kiss on the forehead.

There had been none of the teasing, none of the sexual overtones, not even a repeat of the brief kiss that had occurred between the two of them after they had left Madame Olivetti's that first time. It was obvious, thought Nicki, Eric saw her only as a child. But she was determined that tonight he would see her as a woman—a warm, desirable woman! Hence, the small fortune she had spent for the black evening gown. She knew it made her look her very best, accentuating the lovely curves of her figure.

Nicki slipped into the dress and was attempting to zip the long back zipper when Maude Benson strolled into the girl's bedroom amid the heavy aroma of French perfume and the soft swirl of aqua chiffon and dyed mink.

"Would you like some help with that, my dear?" asked her aunt. "Bill and I do hate to run out on you again, but it's Wally Stanton's testimonial dinner tonight and Bill promised ages ago that he'd give the keynote speech. It's going to be dreadfully dull, I'm afraid. I would much rather be going with you and Eric," she sighed. "There, you're all done up now," announced the older woman as she stepped back to study the lovely girl before her, sensuous in the clinging black gown. Maude was suddenly reminded that her niece was no longer a child, but a beautiful woman.

"Nicki . . ." she began hesitantly. "I-I don't know if you'll consider me a busybody for saying this. I mean I do realize you're almost twenty-one years old, but I believe

51

if Abigail were alive and here now she would feel it her maternal duty to warn you about a—a man like Eric Damon. You've spent a great deal of time together this past week or so." Her aunt took a deep breath and plunged on. "I'm not putting this very well, am I? I haven't had much practice at this kind of thing, I'm afraid. Look, Nicki, Eric is charming, wealthy, and far too attractive for his own good. He is used to getting whatever he wants. Be careful, darling, please! He's much more experienced than you are and no one wants to see you get hurt."

"Oh, Aunt Maude, you are a dear," reassured Nicki with a light-hearted laugh as she gave her aunt a hug. "Eric treats me like a child. There's no reason for you to worry! He's been the perfect gentleman, the kind bachelor uncle. He doesn't see me like—like that." She colored as she spoke the last few words.

"I suppose you're right, Nicki. It's just that you seem so grown-up all of a sudden. You've become a lovely woman, my dear," her aunt remarked thoughtfully.

"Coming from a woman who is renowned for her beauty, that means a great deal to me. Thank you, Maude," Nicki replied sincerely. "Now I don't want you and Uncle Bill to worry about me. Just go have a good time tonight." She was still reassuring the two of them as they exited several minutes later.

Bustling back to her room, the young woman opened the bottom drawer of her bureau and extracted a box wrapped in silver foil. It contained her gift for Eric Damon —an exquisite silver cigarette lighter from Tiffany's, with his initials engraved on the front. She knew it was the perfect gift for a woman to give a man. And Nicki meant to present it to Eric at the end of their evening, when he brought her back to the apartment and they were all alone.

"And what do I want to happen then?" asked the girl

out loud. Would Eric bestow a kiss on her cheek as he said thank you? Or would he gather her into his arms and kiss her with all the passion she suspected burned just beneath his cool exterior? The young woman blushed furiously at her own daydreams. What was happening to her? Why must she make Eric see her as a woman, a real woman?

"Because he treats you like a first-form schoolgirl, a silly, young schoolgirl who doesn't know the first thing about men or what it means to be a real woman. And it's not true!" She answered her own question. "You are a woman, Nicole Swithin—with a woman's emotions and feelings and longings. And tonight the whole world can know it, for all I care, just as long as Eric does."

It was his kindly attitude that irritated her, that drove her to pound her fist into the bed pillow out of sheer frustration, she said to herself. That very first night in the study he had asked her if she had ever wondered what it would be like to be kissed by a man like him. She had fearfully told him "no." But that was years ago and now she could confess, at least to herself, that her answer had changed and it was a definite "YES." She wanted very much to be kissed by Eric Damon. It was partly curiosity and partly because he was the best-looking man she had ever known, and she was just a little bit in love with him.

"But you've got to be careful," whispered Nicki to her reflection in the floor-length mirror in front of her. "This is no child's game you're playing. This is Eric Damon's kind of game and if you're not careful it's for keeps!"

A harsh buzzing abruptly cut off her daydreaming. She placed the giftbox on the small oak bed table and went to answer the doorbell, knowing it would be the man who was so much in her thoughts.

And there he stood—the elegant linen dinner jacket the perfect contrast for his jet-black hair streaked at the temples. He was casually leaning against the door frame, smoking his usual cheroot, smoky blue eyes taking in every inch of the fair creature poised in the open doorway, a tentative smile touching the corners of her red mouth.

"You've never looked lovelier, Nicki," he drawled through his teeth. "Nor more tempting. Are 'you' going to be my surprise birthday present?" he murmured lazily.

A quiver of excitement ran through the girl. It would seem that her dress was already having the desired effect. Eric hadn't teased her like this since that first meeting, only then there had been a streak of cruelty in his manner. It was missing now.

"Why, Mr. Damon, don't tell me you've never been given a girl for your birthday before?" she teased him back.

"Absolutely never! Why don't you ask me in for a drink, Nicki? We have plenty of time before dinner and I feel like celebrating," he suggested in a noncommittal tone.

"Sure, only you'll have to tell me how to mix whatever it is you want because I'm still an amateur. I've just learned the difference between a martini and a manhattan," she confessed with a chuckle. "Uncle Bill thinks I may be hopeless as a bartender. It all tastes medicinal to me!" she said, making a face.

"In that case, I'll help myself. I know where Bill keeps my favorite brand of bourbon and I'm not turning a beginner loose on that," he said as he sauntered into the living room of the Bensons' apartment ahead of her.

Nicki followed him, thinking how natural he looked in the luxurious surroundings she had found so awe-inspiring upon her arrival. The cream-colored sofas and love seats accented with chocolate-brown throw pillows, the exquisite "objets d'art," the windows that reached from floor to ceiling and led to the greenhouse beyond—it had all been outside the realm of her experience. Yet now it almost seemed homey in a familiar sort of way. She had never dreamt she would ever feel that way about any place besides their home in Cheswick. And could it really have been less than a fortnight since her plane had landed at Kennedy Airport? It seemed a lifetime ago.

She looked up as Eric spoke to her. "Are you having anything?"

She shook her head no and thoughtfully sank down into one of the love seats situated on either side of the fireplace. The dark-haired man chose to remain standing, gazing down at her in silence. Nicki suddenly found herself tongue-tied. Tonight was different and he was as much aware of it as she was. Nicki was acutely conscious of the expensive cologne he wore, mingled with the aroma of his cigar. She had never been so physically aware of a man before in her life. It was suddenly quite frightening.

"A penny for your thoughts," he finally asked her in a quiet voice.

"What? Oh—was I wool-gathering again? I'm sorry, did you say something?"

"I wondered when you'll be leaving for Maine," he repeated.

"Maine? I-I'd almost forgotten," she murmured. "I suppose I must be going in four or five days. My cousins are expecting me, you know," she explained unnecessarily.

"I'll be leaving New York soon myself," he offered matter-of-factly.

"Y-you will?" She tried desperately to sound nonchalant, but the slightest quiver crept into her voice despite all her efforts. "Where will you be going—or do you mind if I ask?" She suddenly remembered what he had said to Nadine during that telephone conversation the first night.

She mustn't make that same mistake. This man answered to no one.

"I'll be attending an economic conference in Paris next week," he said blandly.

"You'll enjoy Maine," he added a moment later. "It can get depressingly hot in New York in July and August. Maine will be much more to your liking then. An excellent opportunity to see some of small-town America—to meet some hardworking, normal people." He emphasized his words with a positive nodding of his head. "Yes, you'll like Maine."

"I assume you've been there since you so confidently extol its virtues," Nicki stated dryly, raising one eyebrow in a question. "You've traveled to a great many places, haven't you, Eric?"

"Yes to both questions," he answered smoothly.

"I-I haven't been much of any place until this trip, but I suppose I've already told you that in my own rambling fashion," Nicki said with a funny little smile. "It never mattered to me, until now. There's a lot more than just a few years separating us, isn't there, Eric?" She was suddenly very serious.

"I'm afraid so," Eric replied gently, his blue-gray eyes studying her with quiet intensity. "Perhaps we'd better be going, Nicki."

"All right, just let me run get my shawl," she sighed, a trace of melancholia in her voice. She stopped before the mirror in her bedroom and stared at the shadowed eyes of the girl before her. The past ten days had been a sweet dream, a dream that was soon to be over. Now the harsh reality was crashing down around her. It was at that precise moment that she knew—she was in love with Eric Damon! And after next week she would never see him again.

* * *

Nicki pirouetted dreamily, cheeks pink with excitement and champagne, hazel eyes closed. She put her arms around the man's neck and softly hummed the love song they seemed to have danced to all evening.

"It was a gorgeous evening, Eric," she said in a low, throaty voice as he disengaged himself and took her key to unlock the apartment door. "Every girl should have one perfect night like tonight to remember all of her life. I feel like it was my birthday and Christmas all rolled into one."

"I'm glad you enjoyed yourself," the man said, an amused smile spreading across his tanned features. He took the girl's elbow to steady her as he guided her into the apartment.

"Would you like a brandy?" she asked politely.

"Perhaps we ought to skip the brandy and have a cup of coffee," he suggested.

"Oh, no," Nicki pouted prettily. "I don't want to lose this marvelous feeling now. Don't be a party pooper, my dear man. Let's sit here with the lights turned low and sip our Grand Marnier while we watch the lights of Manhattan and whisper to each other the deepest secrets in our souls." A small giggle escaped.

"Nicole Swithin, I do believe you are just a little intoxicated," he speculated with an indulgent expression in his blue eyes.

"You may be right, Mr. Eric Damon, financier, world traveler, man-about-town—any town, but it's not the champagne, it's New York that has me feeling so high. It's the sense of expectation, the bright lights, the masses of people down there. What girl wouldn't be walking with her feet a few inches off the ground? It's a balmy summer evening and I've just taken a hansom cab ride through Central Park with a devastatingly handsome man. Now I

57

ask you—what girl could resist all that and not feel intoxicated?"

Eric chuckled, shaking his head. "I hope you never lose your enthusiasm for living, little one. Let's drink a toast to youth and the incredible zest the young have for living," he proposed as he raised his glass of amber liquid to hers.

"And I wish you a happy birthday," she responded in turn, gazing up into his face as if searching for some clue, some hint of his real feelings. But the inscrutable mask was firmly in place.

"Oh, my gosh," Nicki exclaimed jumping up. "I almost forgot your present. Don't go away!" And before Eric knew what was happening, the girl had dashed from the room.

Once in her bedroom, Nicki scooted her skirt up over her knees so she could hunch down and open the bottom bureau drawer, ransacking its lacy contents as she frantically searched for the giftbox.

"Damn! Damn!" she muttered in frustration. "What did I do with it?"

"Tut, tut, is that any way for a proper young lady to talk?" came a sarcastic male voice from directly above her.

"I don't care. I can't find it. I can't find my present for you," she cried out softly. She straightened up to face the tall lithe man now only inches away. "And please remove that ridiculous grin from your face, Mr. Damon. I don't think it happens to be very funny!" she spat out at him like an enraged creature.

"I adore the way your eyes blaze bright green when you're indignant with me," Eric rubbed in. "It brings back such sweet memories of our first meeting."

"Hrrrmph." Her head was tossed back, cheeks aflame, eyes glistening, ready to do battle.

"By the way, the missing tribute wouldn't be in a small silver Tiffany's box, would it?" he added slyly.

"W-why, how did you know?" Nicki asked in bewilderment. Eric took her shoulders into his strong, muscular hands and turned her around to face the bedtable.

"Of course! I had it out earlier and when you rang the buzzer I must have put it down. How silly of me," she reprimanded herself primly. "Well, h-happy birthday, Eric, and thank you for everything," she said fervidly, handing him the box.

Eric took it from her hands without touching her, yet a shiver still ran through the young woman as he continued to stand there staring down at her with a strange light in his eyes. Then it was gone and Eric casually flopped down on the pink comforter and unloosened his tie with one hand while he patted the bed next to him with the other.

"Keep me company while I open my present. We might as well be comfortable," he said nonchalantly.

"All right," answered Nicki, accepting his unvoiced challenge as she eased herself down on the bed next to his reclining form.

"The lighter is perfect, thank you, Nicki," he commented after a few moments. Turning over onto his back he stared up at the lovely blond woman in the black gown. "You look very much like a soft, loving woman tonight, Nicki," he said off-handedly.

"I am a woman, Eric."

"In that case, come here, Nicki—take pity on this poor man you see before you. Bestow a birthday kiss upon this furrowed brow," he was teasing her lightly, but the laughter never reached his watchful eyes.

She hesitated, nervously running her tongue along her bottom lip.

"Surely you aren't afraid of me. Or are you?" he pursued. "Nicki?"

"Of course not!" scoffed the girl with false bravado. Wasn't this the very thing she had dreamed of? she asked herself silently.

Nicki bent over the reclining form of the man as he lay there motionless, her soft lips brushed the hard line of his jaw, her own breathing suddenly erratic.

He caught her then as she straightened up and pulled her back down on the bed beside him.

"Eric?" her whole being questioned him.

"Hush, woman! Put your arms around me. Kiss me, Nicki. You know as well as I do that it's what we both want!" he commanded in a husky voice as he lowered his mouth to hers. "Forget everything but the two of us."

He kissed her then, a gentle exploratory kiss that promised to be only a prelude to passion. It was obvious even to Nicki that Eric was trying to keep a firm hold on his own rising excitement. He waited for the merest sign from the young, warm creature in his embrace, a sign that she desired him as much as he wanted her.

Raising his head slightly, he peered down into the girl's lovely flushed face. "Nicki?"

"Oh, come here, darling," she murmured, tugging at his sleeve.

Then Eric's hot urgent mouth was parting her trembling lips, seeking the sweet moistness within. Nicki's mouth began to move under his, opening wildly to accept him. The world slipped away as she felt a violent stirring deep within her. All the girl knew was that this iron-hard, passionate man wanted her and that her own awakening desires were surging like a tidal wave to answer his. Eric elicited a primitive response from Nicki that she never dreamt herself capable of. She was quite sure she had never felt like this before in her life.

His strong hands moved sensuously down her slender back, exploring the soft curves, teaching her body to respond to him. Pulling her roughly onto his chest, he pressed her thighs against his own hard form. With a tortured groan, Eric gathered a mass of blond curls in his fist, burying his burning face in the hollow of her throat.

"Oh, God, Nicki, I don't know how I've kept away from you for so long! Always being near you, aching to touch you. I want you as badly as I've ever wanted any woman in my life. What am I going to do about you?" he muttered against her creamy skin.

"Please, Eric, I-I love you! Please kiss me again," she whispered a little desperately as his mouth willingly descended on hers.

As if by their own volition, the girl found her hands trying to reach the firm flesh beneath Eric's silk shirt. He freed one of his own hands from its exploration long enough to help the trembling girl pull the material free of his trousers. Then Nicki tentatively let her small, tremulous fingers roam over the steely muscles of his damp back.

Eric gathered her into his arms, bringing her closer and closer until Nicki could feel every bone and muscle of the man straining against her. Somewhere in the back of her mind she realized that the zipper of her evening gown had been undone, but before she could utter a word of protest, Eric had pushed the black brocade from her shoulders and was caressing her with his lips.

Leaving a trail of burning kisses across her bare flesh, he sought the spot below her ear before lowering his head to the firm roundness of her breast. Nicki unconsciously arched her back, pressing against him, unknowingly provocative in her movements. The man murmured her name in a harsh whisper, without meaning to speak aloud. He urgently pushed aside the lacy material and caught the hardened nipple between his teeth, his passion now fully aroused.

"Eric!"

She cried out his name and their burning mouths came together once more as if they would never get enough of the other even if they lived ten lifetimes. The man rolled over, never taking his hungry mouth from hers, covering her bareness with his own body, pressing her down into the bed.

"I, for one, am very glad this evening is over," yawned Bill Benson as he draped his arm affectionately around his wife's shoulder. "It's good to be home, Maude. I know it was a tedious evening for you, but somehow you always manage to look lovely, to act interested at these functions. How ever you do it, my dear, I thank you!"

Maude rested her head against the sturdy shoulder of the fiftyish man close at her side. "I would do anything for you, darling," the woman sighed contentedly.

"I know, Maude," he said with a tender smile. "Will you have a nightcap with me?"

"I think I'll check on Nicki first, dearest, but I'll only be a moment. I wonder how her evening with Eric went?" she said half to herself. "Bill—you don't think Nicki's fallen for him, do you?" There was genuine concern in her voice as she turned toward her husband.

"Now, now, Maude. You worry too much. Damon has more sense than to let anything happen even if Nicki doesn't. But in my opinion, our niece is a young woman with both feet firmly on the ground," Bill Benson reassured his spouse.

Moments later Maude was tapping lightly on the door to Nicki's bedroom. "Nicki . . . are you still awake?" she called out in hushed tones as she turned the knob to enter. "How was your evening? . . . Oh, my God—Eric!" Maude Benson froze, her eyes suddenly wide with shock. "Oh, no, not Nicki!" she cried out in distress.

Eric recovered some measure of composure first. He turned his head to answer the older woman while still shielding the girl's state of dishevelment from the eyes of her aunt.

"I-It's all right, Maude. Go—out into the other room, please," he growled in a raspy tone. "I-I'll be there in a minute. Just go!"

"A-all right," she was finally able to respond shakily as she turned to let herself out of the room.

"Oh, Nicki . . ." he moaned, resting his forehead on hers for a moment. She lay there, eyes closed, tears forming on her thick golden lashes. A long, drawn-out sigh issued from the quivering lips so close to his own.

"I'm sorry, little one," he murmured dimly, his warm breath fanning her reddened cheeks. "I-I'd give anything if this hadn't happened. Dammit! I lost control! Something I never allow myself to do. It was my fault, Nicki." He spoke in a quiet voice, reproaching himself with every word.

"I'd better go reassure Maude and Bill that no irreparable damage has been done." Her tear-filled eyes flew open at the stinging sarcasm in his voice. A painful expression flitted across her soft features.

"W-wouldn't it be better if we faced them together?" She hardly dared to breathe, afraid to put her hopes into words.

"No, little one. Right now it's better if I face the music alone. You pull yourself together before you come out.

You have the soft, vulnerable look of a woman who's just been made love to—a fact your aunt and uncle are bound *not* to appreciate." Dark humor slipped back into his manner.

"We—we've got to talk. Don't we?" she asked tensely.

"Later." He pulled himself away from the girl and stood up to straighten his clothing into some semblance of order. Shivering with the sudden loss of his warmth, Nicki wrapped her arms around herself, watching his every movement through heavy-lidded eyes.

"I'll take care of everything with your aunt and uncle, honey. Don't you worry," he said brusquely. "Are you going to be all right, Nicki?"

She fought to sound casual as she answered, "Yes. . . . "Eric—I—I do love you," came the quiet confession.

Long brown fingers tore through his black hair in agitation. "I know. That's the hell of it, Nicki. That's the real hell of it!" And then he was gone, leaving her all alone.

It was some minutes before Nicki was composed enough to consider moving from the spot where Eric had left her lying. She finally sat up and began to rectify her tousled appearance. Turning abruptly, she caught a vision of her rumpled, partially clad body in the mirror.

Oh, God, she cried to herself, pressing her eyes tightly shut to stop the flow of tears, to think she had nearly lost her head and allowed Eric Damon to make love to her. Who are you kidding, Nicki, you did lose your head, face it! But somehow she couldn't bring herself to wish that tonight had never happened. She loved Eric, madly and completely, and she was very sure that he wanted her too. She wouldn't think any further than that, she told herself. Not now, anyway.

Nicki straightened the lines of her black sheath and

vigorously brushed her hair until her arms ached for her to stop. Then she applied fresh lip gloss and a touch of powder as if they would cover up the dreamy, faraway look in her eyes. A gentle rap at her door drew her attention as she was checking herself from head to toe in the full-length mirror.

"Nicki—? It's Maude. May I come in?"

"O-of course," the girl called out in a tentative voice. "Oh, Aunt Maude!"

"My dear Nicki!"

The two women spoke simultaneously, gazing at each other across the wide expanse of pink carpeting.

"I . . . was just coming to join you . . . you and Uncle Bill and Eric, I mean," Nicki went on, her voice low and husky.

"Sit down, Nicki," her aunt suggested kindly. "I *must* talk to you."

The girl perched herself on the edge of the bed while Maude furiously paced the floor. "Nicki—Eric has gone." Maude finally paused in front of her niece as she made the announcement. "He—he asked that Bill and I say good-bye to you on his behalf. You'll be leaving for Maine soon and he for Paris—and he felt it was best that you not see each other again. Under the circumstances, your uncle and I heartily agreed. We don't blame you one bit for what nearly happened in this apartment tonight, my dear. Eric Damon alone is held accountable for that! It's best this way, believe me, Nicki!" Her aunt seemed to be pleading for the girl's understanding, her tone matching the despair of her countenance.

She went on. "Eric Damon is an international playboy —he made his first million at twenty-one and has been with dozens of glamorous, sophisticated women ever since —he doesn't marry his women, Nicki! Your uncle and

65

I—we don't want you to get caught up in that kind of life. We love you too much to stand by and watch that man break your heart!" The tears were unashamedly streaming down Maude Benson's face as she finished.

Every semblance of color had drained from Nicki's face. She sat immobile, trying desperately to comprehend what the other woman was telling her.

Never see each other again! Nicki shook her head in disbelief. There had to be a mistake—some terrible mistake. She was in love with Eric. He had made love to her and she had responded with her heart in her eyes, and in her hands and lips. Now Maude was telling her that he had left, charging her aunt to say his farewells!

"No!" The protest was wrenched from the very center of the girl's being.

"What is it, dear? What's wrong?" her aunt choked through her tears.

The young woman stared at Maude Benson, startled and hurt. "This can't be the end, not after tonight. Oh, dear God, help me—I'm in love with the man!" She murmured so quietly that the older woman could barely hear her.

"I'm sorry, my dear, truly I am. But you've known Eric such a short time. This infatuation will pass and then you'll realize just how lucky you were to escape with only your feathers singed," Maude concluded with forced cheerfulness.

"I-I think it's too late to escape." Nicki's voice thickened momentarily. "I've never felt like this before, Maude, and I'm very much afraid that I'm really in love with Eric Damon. D-don't tell me how foolish that is. No one knows that better than I. I think I know the kind of woman I am—and I know what kind of man Eric is and the two don't go together. That's all there is to it! Sometimes he actually frightens me and then there are times when I don't like him at all . . . but I don't think that's going to help me to stop loving him." Her voice was barely a whisper.

"Then I can only say how sorry I am for the hurt I've brought on you."

"Don't be silly, Aunt Maude. You didn't bring any of this on me! I'm an adult now, not a little girl," she reminded her worried relation. "Hey, you look tired, why don't you go to bed? We can always talk in the morning."

"A-all right, dear. I am suddenly quite weary," confessed her aunt as she bent to touch her lips to the young woman's forehead. "Try to get some sleep, Nicki. Things will look differently to you in the morning."

"Good night, Maude," Nicki answered tonelessly, her mind already racing ahead to her own thoughts.

The metallic click of the door handle signaled Maude Benson's withdrawal from the room. Nicki threw herself back against the mound of pink and red pillows. Her gaze flitted from one object to another, reflecting the emotional turmoil she felt.

Turning her head sharply to check the clock on the bedside table, a small shiny object snagged on the satin bedcover caught her eye—Eric's lighter! The silver cigarette lighter she had chosen with such loving care for his birthday—he had left it behind! Nicki carefully untangled it and held the cold metal against her burning face.

"Oh, Eric," she whispered bleakly, "did I mean so little to you?" The tears were on the verge of flowing once again.

Wait a minute, Nicki, she said to herself. This wallowing in a mire of self-pity is not only useless, but premature as well. The man was certainly not indifferent to her, any more than she was to him. He had almost begun a love affair with her, not ended one. Why would he walk out without a word of explanation, that was what she didn't understand. Unless it was Maude and Bill's doing. Then she laughed out loud at her own feeble attempts to analyze a man like Eric Damon. He was out of her league. He did exactly what he liked, he was a law unto himself. There was only one way for her to find out where she stood with Eric Damon—she must return the lighter to him herself.

"You'll only make a fool of yourself," she warned the blue-eyed creature in the mirror. "But does it really matter even if you do?" she whispered. "You've got to find out what's going on—and first thing in the morning you'll do exactly that!"

CHAPTER FOUR

The next morning at eight o'clock sharp a pale, dark-eyed slip of a girl was nervously placing her request to see Eric Damon before a third security official at the exclusive Fifth Avenue address.

"All right, miss," the uniformed guard finally conceded, "I'll ring the penthouse, but you better be on the level about knowing Mr. Damon or we'll both be in hot water."

"Please—just call Mr. Damon, it'll be all right, you'll see," she reassured him.

He returned several minutes later, absorbed in selecting a key from the large ring attached to his gunbelt.

"Okay, Miss Swithin, if you'll follow me, please, I'll unlock the penthouse elevator for you. It only connects with Mr. Damon's floor so if you'll just step inside. Wait until it stops then exit from the elevator and proceed straight ahead to the large red double doors. Mr. Damon is expecting you."

"Thank you," she responded a little absently, thinking ahead to her uncertain meeting with Eric.

Three minutes later the young woman found herself poised in front of the lacquered Chinese-red doors denoting the penthouse. Raising her hand to press what she thought was a door chime, she jumped visibly when the door flew open before her.

"Hello, Nicki." It was Eric—unshaven, his usually immaculate hair rumpled; obviously still laboring his way out of sleep. His only garment was a short velour bathrobe that left his lean muscular legs and bare feet revealed.

"Hello, Eric. I-I woke you up." It was a statement rather than a question. "I'm sorry!" She stood there shifting her weight from one sandaled foot to the other, looking incredibly fresh and young. Unable to meet his eyes, she studied a spot somewhere over his right shoulder.

"Come on in. I don't know about you, but I need a cup of coffee. Williams must have some made in the kitchen." He turned and sauntered down a hallway, obviously expecting her to follow him.

She paused momentarily and then trotted along behind him, catching a glimpse of an exquisite, modern living room replete with large green potted plants and stark, brass furniture. His penthouse was just as Nicki thought it might be—expensive, something out of an interior decorator's notebook, very masculine, and without a single personal touch. Eric had mentioned that he used this apartment for business, it was obviously not his home.

Finding him no longer in view ahead of her, Nicki hurried along the corridor into a bright, cheerful kitchen. One wall was covered in wallpaper of vibrant yellow, orange, and apple-green stripes while the opposite end of the room was a bold plaid done in coordinated colors. Copper pots and utensils were hung everywhere, giving an impression of artistic clutter. There were two large enameled ovens built into the walls as well as a microwave and a charcoal-less barbecue. Every modern convenience had been included in this chef's dream of a kitchen.

"It's fantastic!" breathed Nicki.

"What?" Eric asked as he extracted two coffee mugs from the cupboard above his head.

"I said, this kitchen is fantastic!"

"Yes, I suppose it is," he said lamely. Pouring the hot dark liquid into the awaiting mugs he pushed one along the counter toward her. "From your appreciative gaze, may I assume that you are fully domesticated—or at the very least, that you pursue the culinary arts?"

"If, in your own clever way, you're asking if I can cook, then the answer is 'yes.' As a matter of fact, I'm an excellent cook," she stated flippantly. "But it just so happens, I've never seen a kitchen like this one before outside of a magazine. It is impressive, Mr. Damon."

"Then that is a shame since this one gets so little use. I almost exclusively entertain in restaurants or have food sent in. The kitchen, like the whole apartment, is strictly for convenience and show."

"Where do you really live, Eric?" she asked, suddenly quiet.

"I thought I'd told you—I have a house in New England, an apartment in London . . ."

"You know that's *not* what I meant."

"Look, Nicki, you didn't wake me up at eight o'clock on a Saturday morning to discuss my place of residence."

"Obviously not!" she answered shortly as she plopped herself down on a high-legged bar stool beside him. She had not been this close to him physically since the night before. His very nearness sent a shiver through her.

"Well, then?" His impatience was written across his face.

"If you're trying to make this as difficult as possible for

me, I assure you, you're succeeding!" she cried out sharply. After a heavy pause, she went on. "A-actually, I came here this morning to return your cigarette lighter. It seems you left it behind last night—in your rush."

"All right, Nicki," he sighed wearily. "Look, I had a very short night. I'd like a shave and a shower and then we can talk."

She shook her head in agreement, her blond waves moving to and fro about her face. "And I'll back up my earlier boast by cooking you a first-rate breakfast." She looked up at him as he rose to his feet.

"Oooo, child—don't look at me with those big puppy-dog eyes of yours. If you were any younger, I could be charged with contributing to the deliquency of a minor!" He stopped behind her, reaching out a hand to smooth the windblown strands of honey-colored hair. The surprising tenderness of his touch started her trembling again.

"I'll be back in twenty minutes," he repeated softly.

It was nearly a half hour later when Eric reentered the kitchen, showing no signs of his earlier fatigue, his grooming once more immaculate. He was wearing close-fitting black trousers and a black silk shirt left open at the neck. Nicki was sure he could hear her heart pounding from where he stood. She could make out small beads of water on the dark hair smattered across his bronzed chest, a gold medallion nestled there.

"Breakfast is served, sir." She forced the gay nonchalance into her voice; her throat actually felt painfully constricted. "I hope you don't mind, Eric—I just opened up cupboards and snooped!"

"I don't mind," he said quietly. "It looks good, but I think I'll hold my verdict in abeyance until I've had a chance to taste it," he teased her lightly as she set down

72

in front of him a plate heaped with ham, scrambled eggs, and toasted muffins.

"If I'd had the time and the necessary ingredients, it would have been a proper English breakfast."

"You certainly turned out to be a domestic soul."

"I *can* be when I want to," she corrected him. "I can also do several dozen things rather well that have nothing to do with being domestic! Why is it men are always so damned surprised when a professional woman or an artist or an intellectual shows some domestic skill as well? As if one talent excluded all others!"

"Here she goes again, folks," he muttered.

"No, I'm serious, Eric. That kind of thinking really burns me up! I'm an artist in several fields—I'm a pianist, and I even compose a little; I've had several poems published by respected literary journals. And I have some business know-how as well. I can type, take dictation, balance accounts, and keep impeccable files. But just because I do those things well, men expect me to be lost in a kitchen. Well, I'm not! And what's more I can knit and crochet and I have a green thumb when it comes to growing things." She only paused because she was out of breath.

"Is all this on your resume?" he chuckled.

She suddenly laughed along with him in a high happy chirpy voice.

"I don't know what it is about you, my dear man, but you make me feel on the defensive and the next thing I know I'm up on my soapbox again."

"Sometimes that's the way it is between two people— they may rub each other the wrong way or the right way, but there's never just indifference between them. Now, you better eat your breakfast before it gets cold," he reminded her gently. "I'll get us another cup of coffee—or would you prefer tea?"

"Well . . . actually, I'd rather have tea, but I can get it."

"Nonsense, you're not the only one with hidden domestic talents. I happen to make an excellent cup of tea myself."

She was polishing off her second cup when it suddenly hit Nicki that she'd been enjoying herself so much she'd nearly forgotten her purpose in seeking Eric out that morning. But now the hurt and bewilderment of the previous night came flooding back. She glanced up to find him studying her with quiet intensity.

"Why, Eric?"

"Why what, little one?"

"Why did you leave so suddenly last night? H-how could you k-kiss me like that one minute and then just walk away? And to ask Maude and Bill to say good-bye for you, to have someone else tell me that we're never to see each other again! Why couldn't you tell me yourself? I-I never saw you as a coward—as flinching from the task of breaking it off with a woman—not from our first meeting! So why?" She was simply hurt at the first, then she became angry and even sarcastic.

"Look, Nicki, it would never work between you and me, we both know that. First of all, I'm not about to get married. A man like me doesn't make it to the age of thirty-six still a bachelor without a great deal of determination to stay single.

"And then look at you—you're almost half my age, a little wisp of an innocent barely out of the schoolroom. A sweet, young girl who once told me that her dreams were a loving husband and children and a home of her own. We just don't want the same things out of life, Nicki. I don't want to make any commitments to a woman. You

74

wouldn't settle for anything less than marriage. I can't give you what you want, honey. I'd only hurt you!"

"But why didn't you tell me last night? Why run off and leave it to my aunt and uncle?"

"Because I also realize that there's a physical excitement between us—a wildfire that ignites whenever we're around each other. I've never lost control of myself with a woman—I did with you last night. For both our sakes, I've got to stay away from you. Don't you understand that?" He quit talking and rose to his feet. "I-I didn't want to see you again because—because I was afraid of what might happen," he finally conceded, his back to her, the muscles of his torso visibly tensing beneath his shirt.

"Afraid? Of what? I can't imagine you being afraid of anything," she said softly as she moved to stand beside him.

"Well, I am—and if you had any sense you would be too!" he spat fiercely as he spun around to face her. "And stop being so damned provocative!"

"I-I'm not." She choked back the sudden tears.

"You are—but you can't help it," Eric groaned close to her ear. "Hair the color of wild honey, long slender legs, a lovely young body that most women would sell their souls for. Sometimes—sometimes, I wish I'd never met you!"

But then his tanned muscular arms could resist no longer, they reached out and pulled her close, his lips hard and urgent on hers, belying the words he had spoken. And when he pried her mouth open with his tongue, Nicki felt her head swirl and the familiar stirrings begin anew. Eric lifted the girl off her feet with complete ease and set her down on the counter top—maneuvering their legs so he could press his own body closer to hers.

Nicki was all soft and pliable beneath his touch, letting

him do what he would with her as his hands strayed to the buttons of her blouse.

"See what I mean?" Eric grated through his teeth. "You let me touch you the way I bet you've never let another man touch you in your life! I think I've had enough experience to know when I'm the first. Why in the hell do you let me? Maude and Bill told me you were as much as engaged to a young man back in England. A guy you've known all of your life, a guy who's crazy about you and wants to marry you. If you love him, how can you allow the intimacies between us? Has he ever kissed you like this or touched you the way I have? I'll bet my life he hasn't! Or have I been all wrong about you—perhaps you do this with all of your men. Have you slept with your Englishman, Nicki? Have you slept with a man?" he demanded in a voice black with anger.

In the tomblike silence of the apartment, the sound of her hand hitting his face echoed like a thunderbolt.

"I hate you!" she shrieked into his face. "I hate you, Eric Damon, more than I ever thought I'd hate or despise anyone—"

"My, my—don't tell me I'm interrupting a lovers' quarrel at this time of the morning?" came the low, sultry voice.

Eric and Nicki both turned, stunned into silence by the sound of a third voice, to see a voluptuous, black-haired woman standing in the kitchen doorway, obviously wearing only the tops to a pair of men's pajamas. Eric's pajamas, thought Nicki, as she saw the monogram on the pocket.

"Evidently, we are destined to always have an audience," he said looking back at Nicki. "And this has to be an historical moment," he continued sarcastically, turning to the other woman. "I didn't realize you even knew there was such a thing as morning, Nadine."

"But of course, darling, it's just that I usually burn the candle at the 'other' end. Think of the times we've wined and dined and made—and danced until dawn." She shuffled into the room, only taking her unnaturally bright eyes off the dark scowling man long enough to see what effect her deliberate slip of the tongue had on the pale girl at his side. She almost nodded visibly to see the girl grow even paler at her insinuation. "Well, now, isn't this cozy? Aren't you going to introduce us, darling?" she purred.

"I should warn you, Nicki, Nadine is on her *best* behavior with you here. She's never been interested in meeting another woman before in her life."

"Since it appears that Eric has forgotten his manners, I'll introduce myself," she said smoothly to the younger woman. "I'm Nadine Cole, an old 'friend' of Eric's. And you must be his latest 'little friend.' She's precious, Eric, but isn't she a little young for you? Or is that the attraction —a vicarious attempt to relive your youth? Does it make you feel seventeen all over again when you hold her in your arms? I wouldn't have thought it of you, darling. You're in perfect physical condition—most men half your age would envy your physique." Her tongue dripped with venom. "By the way, I do hope you've told her the rules of the game the way you play it!"

"Your claws are showing, Nadine. Better sheath them before you get scratched. Nicki may look as meek as a lamb, but she's a tigress in disguise."

"Do you suppose he treats all of his women so contemptuously? Let me see, didn't I hear Eric refer to you as 'Nicki'? Well, we really must get together for lunch one day soon and compare notes. It might be fun. Don't you agree, Nicki?"

"I'm afraid I won't be in New York long enough to accept your 'kind' invitation, Miss Cole. And, no—I can't imagine that we would ever have anything to say to one another," the young Englishwoman retorted with a touch of irony in her voice, having regained part of her natural ginger and wit.

"Hrrmph . . . perhaps you're not quite the baby I imagined. She's really quite lovely, Eric—a bit immature perhaps. But I can see why you were temporarily infatuated with her. I do wonder if she has the expertise to satisfy a man with your appetites. Or is the naiveté strictly an act?"

"You are a bitch, Nadine." He glared in open warfare.

"So you've told me before, lover. But you always keep coming back for more."

"You disgust me! Get your clothes on, Nadine, and get out of my apartment!"

"NO! No, I've got to get away from you two!" hissed Nicki. "It only makes sense that I should be the one to leave." She stopped and pointedly looked up at Eric. "I don't even have to get dressed!" She brushed past the startled pair and marched down the hallway toward the front door.

A long strong arm had her before she could escape. "Nicki!" Eric was directly behind her. "This will inevitably sound like a cliché, but it's not the way it looks."

"Do you know it doesn't even matter to me!" She turned to him with tears of anger and disillusionment in her eyes. "The one I feel sorry for is Nadine. Do you hear me, Eric? I pity that poor, pathetic creature in your kitchen. At least she feels some kind of emotion for you however warped it may be. At least she cares about you enough to fight another woman for you! I heard a bitter

78

man one day on Wall Street say that you were without a heart. I didn't want to believe him then, but it's true. You're successful, clever, ruthless, ambitious—and you're heartless! You don't know how to love. How could I have thought even for a moment that the physical passion between us was love? What a fool I've been!" She skillfully slid from his grasp. Rummaging through her handbag she came up with the silver cigarette lighter, which she casually tossed in his direction. "Good-bye, Eric—and many happy returns!"

The next thing she knew, Nicki was squinting into the bright, blinding sunlight of midmorning.

"Would you like a cab, miss?" the epauletted doorman asked as if he sensed her sudden confusion.

"Y-yes, I suppose so."

His shrill whistle rang out up and down the street in summons. Only moments later a yellow taxicab appeared at the curb, as if it had been conjured up by a sorcerer.

"Where to, lady?" queried the driver.

"I—I don't know. Can you just drive me around f-for a few minutes?"

"Sure, lady, it's your money!" After five minutes of riding in silence, the cabby ventured again. "You're English, aren't you, miss?"

"Yes, I am."

"Always thought an English accent was real classy, myself. Like that's the way English should sound—take Laurence Olivier, for example. Saw him as Hamlet one time years ago. Now that actor fellow could sure talk English! Know what I mean?"

"Yes, I suppose so."

"Look, lady, I don't mean to butt into your business, but don't you have someplace to go? Maybe to a friend's?

79

All this driving around in circles isn't getting you anything but a fare the size of a king's ransom! You must have one friend in New York."

"I do!" cried Nicki with relief. "I should have thought of her before. Can you take me to Woodstock Towers on Forty-second Street?"

"Now you're talking. Sure thing, lady. I'll have you there in no time!" grinned the cabdriver.

Within the space of a few minutes, the young woman found herself at the door of apartment 808, returning the wide smile of pleasure she beheld on Madame Olivetti's face.

"Nicole, what a delightful surprise!"

"Madame, how are you? I hope an unexpected visit won't inconvenience you."

"Not at all, my dear. I was taking care of a little correspondence, but it is unimportant and can wait. Come in." She stepped back graciously to allow the younger woman to enter her apartment. "Would you like a cup of tea?"

"I'd love one! May I help you get it, Madame?"

"No, thank you, child. It's not that I don't appreciate your offer, but it is good for me to keep as active as possible." As she spoke she filled the tea kettle with water and placed it on the stove top. "I make myself use my hands every day in small tasks. Otherwise, I will lose what dexterity I do have. Part of my therapy is knitting, so I've been knitting up a storm! Everyone I know in New York has been presented with a lengthy swatch of my handiwork that I optimistically label a 'scarf.' As a matter of fact, I've started one for you in a golden-hued wool that will match your lovely hair. It takes me quite a while, so you must give me your address in England. I will send it to you once you've returned home." She chuckled to herself and chatted on to the young woman. Then she stopped

80

suddenly and studied Nicki's bowed head. "Why, Nicole —are you crying?"

"Y-yes, Madame," sniffed the girl.

"Would you like to tell me about it?"

"Th-this is so silly. I-I'll be all right in a minute. It was when you mentioned England . . . all of a sudden I felt terribly homesick." She blotted her damp cheeks, but the stream of tears would not stop.

"Are you sure that's all that's upsetting you, dear? I only ask because I've grown quite fond of you and you seemed edgy and unusually pale when you arrived here."

"You're v-very perceptive, Madame."

The auburn-tressed woman moved to sit by the girl on the love seat. She patted the trembling hand that reached out for hers and waited for Nicki's tears to subside.

"Nicki—for whatever reasons we both recognize that a special bond exists between the two of us. I would like it very much if you could bring yourself to call me by my Christian name, Louisa. 'Madame' is so formal."

"If you'd like it, Ma . . . I mean, Louisa, so would I." The girl smiled tremulously.

"May I ask if Eric is the cause of your tears, Nicki?"

"Yes, yes, he is!" It felt good to tell this understanding woman about Eric Damon. "We—we had a big row this morning. He made his position very clear a-and there were some complications and I walked out. Now I'll never see him again, Louisa!"

"And you love him."

"Very much!"

"Then I understand your problem even better than you think. Your lives have been so different—it's as if you and Eric came from different worlds. I'll admit I understand your world far better than the one Eric inhabits. His way of life must often seem shallow and superficial to you, my

81

dear. You've had so many advantages that have been denied to him."

"How strange that you should feel that way, Louisa. Most people would automatically assume I was the disadvantaged one."

"And since when has wealth and all its trappings held any interest for you? No, Nicki, you and I are the lucky ones! We had loving parents; a comfortable, familiar home to grow up in; devoted friends; and—our music."

"You really do understand," exclaimed the girl. "I should have known you would!"

"And then there's Eric—extraordinarily handsome, clever, and wealthy—the poor man. I have watched him for nearly ten years. We first met at the home of a mutual acquaintance. He is not an easy man to know—it would take a good woman a lifetime." She paused to lend emphasis to her words. "Eric reveals so little of himself. One must work to see the real Eric behind the arrogant, proud, self-assured man. His generosity with his money is commendable. He just doesn't know how to share himself. He mistrusts emotion, relies on cold objectivity. I suppose that's one reason he is such a successful businessman."

"And he's never married," thought Nicki out loud.

"True, he has never married. He has escorted a succession of beautiful, sophisticated women over the years. Many would have liked to have become Mrs. Eric Damon, but one was much like the other and he never married. None has touched his heart . . . until now, anyway. I somehow felt with you it would be different."

"Eric told me it just wouldn't work, Louisa. He has no intentions of getting married and he says I'm only the marrying kind."

"And are you?"

"And am I what, Louisa?"

"Are you only the marrying kind?"

"I've always thought so, but when I'm with Eric I forget what kind I am. I just want to love him and have him love me back!" She glowed bright red at the confession.

"Oh, child, you must have put quite a scare into him!"

"I-I don't understand," replied a perplexed Nicki.

"You're a beautiful, desirable young woman, my dear. Warm, tender-hearted, trusting, but with a good practical head on your independent shoulders, as well. I bet Eric has never met the likes of you before in his life." Oddly enough Louisa Olivetti seemed to find something highly amusing.

"But, I'm leaving for Maine on the morning flight and I don't know what to do," cried Nicki in frustration. "What shall I do?" She turned to the older woman with fear in her eyes.

"We, the women who love Eric Damon, must be patient with him," she answered soberly. "Don't you understand, my dear lovely Nicole? He is afraid to love us back. Hasn't Eric told you anything about himself?"

"No," she whispered.

"Eric has never had anyone, Nicki. He grew up in an orphanage that he hated so much that he ran away when he was only fourteen. He has survived by his wits alone in a cold world where only the fittest of the species survive. We mustn't blame him too much for what he has become. We must realize that he has never been taught how to love." Her eyes filled with tears.

"Oh, please, Louisa, don't cry! There was nothing you could have done!" begged Nicki as though her heart were breaking.

"I-I failed him." The older woman wept unconsolably.

"Oh, no, not you," comforted a puzzled Nicki.

"Yes, me—you see, my dear Nicki—I'm Eric's mother!"

Nicki sat stunned.

"B-but—how? Oh, forgive me, Louisa, I didn't mean to say that!" The girl apologized profusely, the shock of Louisa Olivetti's confession registering on her every feature.

"No, no, that's all right. There's no need for you to apologize. Yours was a natural reaction. I-I've told so few people, not because I was ever ashamed but because it wasn't my story to tell. I would like to tell it to you, Nicki. Perhaps it will help you to understand my s-son better. It is a story Eric himself does not know—perhaps one day he will." She paused as if to organize her thoughts.

"It began during the war. I was signed to do a concert tour of England as part of a goodwill mission for the state department. I was performing in London when I met Eric's f-father. He came backstage to tell me how much he enjoyed the concert. He came every night for a week until one night I finally agreed to have a late supper with him. He was a devastatingly handsome man, Nicki, though the ravages of the war had taken their toll. It was a whirlwind courtship and we were married two weeks later. Gabriella Fontini was our honor attendant. I was no dewy-eyed child, but we were supremely happy." Louisa paused and the girl could only imagine the private memories she was reliving.

"You must understand the chaos that existed in Europe at that time. My husband was some years older than I—he had already lost his entire family—father, wife, two children, his home destroyed, his country overrun. He had had so much pain in his life, but he fought on. He was a man of heroic proportions." There was a quiet pride in her

84

voice as she spoke of him again after more than three decades.

"We didn't know how much time we would have together. He was in the underground and I only saw him occasionally after the first few weeks. Th-then he came to me one night, unexpectedly, to tell me . . ." She stopped as if in great pain and took several deep breaths before she could continue. ". . . that his first wife and his two young sons had been miraculously found alive in a refugee camp. There was nothing for us to do—but be strong. There were so many good-byes during the war. Ours was but one. It was only after I returned to New York that I discovered I was going to have a baby. I-I had no one to turn to—I couldn't even tell Eric's father. And then, just before my baby was born I received a cable from Gaby telling me that my—that Eric's father had been killed while on a mission into Denmark. I don't remember much for several months after that. It was some time before the doctors felt I was strong enough to be told that m-my baby had died too." Her voice was so soft that Nicki was forced to move closer to hear the last few words.

"Perhaps someday I will tell you about the years in between, but that is for another time. The thread of my story picks up fifteen years ago when I was teaching at Juilliard and tutoring a few private pupils. I lived in this very apartment. I remember I was having lunch at Stouffer's that day—I picked up a newspaper and there was a face out of my past! Only I knew it couldn't be the man I had loved so many years before in London. It was a photograph of a phenomenal young man who had just astounded the financial community by making several million dollars on the stock market. A young man named Eric Damon! I took that paper home and stuffed it away in a drawer and told myself I was just being fanciful after all

85

these years, that I was seeing something that wasn't there. But I kept taking that paper back out and studying every feature of that so familiar face until I knew I had to do something! So—I went to a very dear friend of mine, a highly respected attorney, and told him my whole story. That's when he delved into past records at the hospital and discovered that my baby had not died. And that Eric Damon was indeed my son!" She got up to refill their teacups, stopping to take a damp cloth and wipe the dusty leaves of the small coleus plant at her elbow.

Without looking up she said, "But how could I walk up to that hard young man and simply announce I was his mother, after all the hurt he had been through? How could I tell him that I didn't even know he was alive until I saw a picture in a newspaper, that he was the image of the father I had loved, that I was only interested in him, that the money was unimportant? I was a woman of modest means and he had just become a very wealthy man. There didn't seem to be any way. So I plotted and planned and learned all I could about Eric Damon—and waited for my chance. And then ten years ago I read that Eric was back in New York and I begged and finagled an invitation through a friend of an acquaintance to a dinner where Eric was to be the guest of honor. That was how and where I finally came face to face with my own son.

"For whatever reasons, we seemed to hit it off well from the first. Since then we see each other whenever he's in town and he sends me lovely and thoughtful gifts from all over the world. It's more than I ever dreamed I would have, Nicki. I don't want to lose that—I have learned not to hope for more."

"Eric told me just before we came to visit you that first time that I was going to meet a very special, a very coura-

86

geous lady . . . even *he* does not know just how courageous!"

"That is a lovely thing to say to an aging woman who has just told you a rather strange story."

"It might make a great difference to Eric if he were to be told the story I have just been privileged to hear," offered Nicki gently.

"Perhaps so." Louisa Olivetti sounded skeptical. "But you must remember that my son is not as 'sympathique' as you, my dear sweet sensitive Nicki. I am not blind to my son's sins—he sees people in terms of what they want from him, because no one has ever given to him with no compensation in mind. To Eric there is always an angle, always an ulterior motive to people's actions. No—it is best that it remain my secret," she sighed.

"How horribly sad, somehow . . . two women who love the same man, each in their own way, one as a mother, one as a lover. And neither can tell him how they feel. In the end, we all three lose," murmured Nicki. "I thank you for telling me your story, Louisa. Sharing your pain has made my own more bearable. I have your secret locked away in my heart and there it will stay."

"Will you write to me while you're in Maine?" The older woman's eyes misted over. "I shall miss you."

"And, I, you, Louisa," replied the girl. "We each share the other's secret. We will never be strangers again."

CHAPTER FIVE

The melodious jingle of the bells attached to the front door alerted Nicki as she meticulously dusted the last row of ceramic pots. She glanced up from her work to see three middle-aged ladies entering the shop. She stopped long enough to call out a cheerful welcome to her first customers of the day.

"Hello, ladies! Would you like to browse for a few minutes or do you have something specific in mind that I could help you with this morning?"

"Good morning, dearie," returned one of the women. "If you could just tell us where we can find the needlepoint kits. We were told that your canvases are all painted."

"The needlepoint is right over here, if you'd care to follow me," said Nicki as she stepped down from the footstool. "Each kit is unique. It includes all the necessary Persian wool to complete the kit and two appropriate needles. As you mentioned, each canvas is hand-painted and one of a kind. My cousin, who owns this shop, creates each design herself. Those are her initials in the corner,

CT, for Clare Trumbull," Nicki explained with pride. Clare was so talented, she thought to herself. It was the most natural thing in the world for her to be enthusiastic with the customers who came into the "White Pine Shop."

"You have so many unusual crafts," commented one of the other women. "I could look all day!"

"We have several dozen local artisans who bring us their work on consignment," Nicki informed them. "For example, every single stitch of these traditional American quilts was sewn by hand. I'm sure you ladies can appreciate the time and skill involved."

"We used to go to quilting bees when we were young marrieds, remember, Hazel?"

"I'm not about to forget, Grace. I must have jabbed myself with a needle hundreds of times. Not all of us were as handy with needle and thread the way you were. My, your fingers fairly flew!"

"Oh, now, don't go boring this young thing with your tales, Hazel," chuckled the third woman. "We know all about those long cold Indiana winters! You go on, miss," she directed Nicki.

"Well, we also have hand-painted hostess skirts, macrame wall hangings and pot slings, our jewelry is crafted by a local silversmith, and we have one family—three generations yet—who whittle all the magnificent wood sculptures you see. We have both crocheted and hand-knitted sweaters and afghans. And the watercolors in the adjoining gallery were done by my cousin's husband— Nash Trumbull. Perhaps you've heard of him—he's one of Maine's leading young painters."

"Why, yes, I do believe I've heard of Nash Trumbull," acknowledged the third woman as she moved closer to Nicki. "Do you suppose we could meet him? It sure would be something to tell the folks back in Seymour!"

"You might catch him in the back of the gallery in the late afternoon. He usually works at this time of the morning, while the light is good. You could check with the gentleman who manages the gallery."

"Annie," called one of her companions. "You must come see these handmade cloth dolls! Why, I had a doll like this when I was just a little girl. It's nearly a lost art now. I didn't know that anyone made these anymore. I must have one to take home."

"Take whatever time you'd like to browse, ladies. If you have any questions my name is Nicki and I'll be happy to help you." Then she graciously withdrew and went back behind the counter to rearrange the leather wallets and handbags. There were so many beautiful things in Clare's shop, thought Nicki. She had been in Bar Harbor only three weeks now and already carefully selected gifts had been mailed home to her father and Gaby and Mark Winstead. She had sent a wood sculpture to Maude and Bill Benson and a crocheted evening sweater to Louisa Olivetti. So far Nicki had been one of the White Pine's best customers!

The tinkling of the bells sent her eyes once again to the door of the craft and hobby shop. This time the girl saw a young man of athletic stature, possessing a pair of vivid green eyes that any woman would be envious of, fair hair bleached fairer by the summer sea and sun, and a quick smile that revealed perfect white teeth. He gave Nicki a wide and welcoming grin.

"Nicki, my love," he greeted the girl as he saunterd toward her. "You look ravishing this morning." He leaned across the counter and planted a quick kiss upon her surprised lips. She did look fetching in tight jeans and a T-shirt embossed with the seal of the state of Maine across the front and the bold black lettering PINE TREE STATE.

"We're going to make you one of us yet!"

"And you, David, are an inveterate flirt!" she laughed. "But the compliments do wonders for my ego."

"A group of us are going horseback riding this afternoon. Why don't you come with us? I've arranged a splendid mount for you named Zephyr, and I know that Clare covers the shop in the afternoons. Come on, Nicki! You can't stick around the house every afternoon practicing your sonatas and scales. All work and no play made 'Jill' a very dull girl. There are a lot of nice kids here for the summer, why don't you come with me and meet some of them? If you don't say yes I'll kiss you again right in front of those three women over by the needlepoint who are watching every move we make with considerable interest. What do you say, Nicki? Give me your answer—quickly!"

"Oh, all right, David," she was finally pressured to agree. "I do love to ride, though it's been a while I must confess."

"You're the first female I've actually had to threaten just to convince her to go out with me. I—I'm not sure you're very good for my ego, Nicki," David pouted with mock injury. "I usually have to fight the girls off."

"I'm sure you do, David. You're a very attractive boy."

" 'Boy'? Hey, you do know how to bring a guy down a rung or two. Well, I've done my homework, Miss Swithin, and it just so happens I'm almost a year older than you are, dear child."

"It's not you, David, honestly. Actually it's me," she said, shaking her blond head, suddenly quite serious. "I-I just couldn't get involved with anyone—not now. It wouldn't be fair to let you become interested in me. I would never be able to feel anything in return."

"So—once bitten, twice shy. And I would say that you've been bitten recently, huh?"

"Something like that, but I'd rather not talk about it."

"And you have a marked preference for older men."

"I wouldn't say that, exactly, but Englishmen seem older somehow than their American counterparts."

"And was 'he' an Englishman?"

"N-no. No, he wasn't."

"Aha, so you do like older men, regardless of nationality. I could always add a few streaks of gray to my temples and perhaps a mustache."

"Now you are being silly. Look, I've got to get back to work. You'd better go," she finally added a little impatiently.

"Okay, Nicki. But I'll meet you at the house after lunch. We'll leave from there. See you later, honey," he called as he loped across the shop to the door. "We're 'kissing cousins,'" he said for the benefit of their audience as he turned back momentarily. "That's the best kind, don't you agree, ladies?"

They twittered among themselves as he left until one woman got her nerve up to speak to Nicki.

"Say, he is a good-looking young man," she commented. "Is he really your cousin?"

"In a distant way, I suppose. That was David Trumbull, Nash Trumbull's younger brother. I guess we're related by marriage—his sister-in-law is my second cousin twice removed or something like that," the girl replied to the curious woman.

"Why, in that case, you're not really related at all," offered the second curious listener. "Is he your young man?"

"Oh, no, we're just friends."

"My, but he is a handsome boy, though."

"Yes, he is a handsome boy," affirmed Nicki.

It was nearly half past one when Nicki and David made their way from Clare and Nash Trumbull's saltbox-style house through the tall grasses that grew between the house and the beach. They raced, laughing, across the dunes to the water's edge. There, two long-legged, jean-clad youths waited on their mounts, the reins to two other riderless horses in their hands.

"Hello!" they called out as they dashed down the beach.

David introduced them casually. "Nicki Swithin—Jenny Stewart and Rod Charles."

"Hi, Nicki," they both greeted her warmly. Jenny was a tallish, slender redhead with a mass of fiery curls and large brown eyes. A ready grin covered her face from her full mouth to her freckled cheeks. Her companion was tall, dark, and good-looking. They both sat poised in the western-style saddles as if it were a totally natural posture.

"We're so glad you could come with us, Nicki," said Jenny. "This is Zephyr. She has spirit but she minds herself. I wasn't sure just how much you'd ridden and Dave didn't seem to know, so I picked a horse you could count on." The explanation was given as Nicki swung herself up into the saddle. David double-checked the cinch and stirrups for her and then they were ready to be off.

"Thanks! She seems perfect for me, Jenny. I'm so happy to be here!" And Nicki was sincere.

Without further ado the four riders turned their mounts around and walked them along the beach until the young golden-haired girl felt comfortable with the chestnut mare beneath her. It was a perfect summer day on Mt. Desert Island—blue skies, white cotton clouds, and a tangy sea breeze. Cool waves lapped at the horses' fetlocks, their hoof prints erased from the sand almost in the same moment they lifted one hoof to put it down again farther along the beach. Nicki felt the salty breeze move through her hair, the warmth of the sun full upon her face. She closed her eyes for a moment to breathe it all in and a sense of peacefulness descended on her being. For the first time since meeting Eric Damon, she felt free and wild again.

"Glad you came?" a quiet voice asked beside her.

"It's wonderful! How could I have forgotten the sense of freedom you find when it's only you and a horse?"

"Now aren't you glad I insisted you come away with us this afternoon?"

"Yes, oh yes, David!"

Rod turned back and called over his shoulder, obviously for Nicki's benefit, "The shoreline starts getting fairly rugged up ahead so we'll be leaving the beach and heading inland. There are plenty of excellent trails just south of us in Acadia National Park."

"We'll come over one afternoon next week and take one of the scheduled oceanside nature hikes given by the park rangers," suggested David. "You can't spend the summer on Mt. Desert Island without taking in all the local sights, including Cadillac Mountain, which rises over fifteen hundred feet above sea level. Then we'll indulge ourselves in the local dishes—steamed clams, lobster dripping with drawn butter, corn on the cob. Just think of it, girl, we offer beautiful scenery; glorious summer weather, without air-conditioning; delectable, mouth-watering seafood; warm and friendly, very friendly, people—what more could you ask for?"

"I don't know about you, Nicki, but he's succeeded in making me very hungry!" laughed Jenny.

Nicki smiled at the young man riding beside her, hoping he did not see the sudden flash of pain in her eyes, brought on by his question. Yes, indeed, what more could a girl ask for? —Just the love of the man she loves, thought Nicki. Don't . . . don't think about him, she scolded herself. She had found some measure of contentment since coming to Maine, though she admitted Eric Damon was never long absent from her thoughts. At first, she had cried herself to sleep every night until she felt wrung dry, unable to ever shed another tear. Ugly dark circles appeared beneath her cloudy blue-green eyes and a loss of appetite left her clothes noticeably larger. She was finally forced to take stock of her situation. She could not go on this way—for one thing it wasn't fair to her cousin Clare.

And Clare and Nash Trumbull had turned out to be the best kind of people—down-to-earth, thoughtful of her privacy. They had graciously opened up their home to their young English cousin. Her bedroom was big and bright and faced the ocean. It was filled with antiques and had its own adjoining bath, besides—a delightful room with a high, old-fashioned bed complete with a needlepointed footstool and a coverlet crocheted of cotton thread, a cedar chest poised at its foot, a dark pine bookcase laden with reading material to suit every taste, and a granny rocker by the window.

And Nicki soon thoroughly enjoyed her mornings in the White Pine Shop, her afternoons at the grand piano in the front parlor, or taking long walks along the beach, adding to her recently acquired seashell collection. It was little wonder that this island had been a popular summer resort area since the end of the nineteenth century: the squall of the gulls overhead, the peaceful monotony of one wave coming in to shore after another, the bright sun above, and ocean as far as the eye could see. Off in the distance, rising above the tops of even the tallest pines, was a telltale chimney—one of the many magnificent homes that dotted the island, despite a disastrous forest fire over thirty years ago that nearly destroyed all of Bar Harbor, reducing numerous estates to blackened ashes.

They were trotting single file now along a well-worn bridle path that wound through a forested area of the park. Jenny took the lead, followed by Rod, then Nicki and David. Sunlight filtered down through the thick lush growth of pine trees. It was cooler here and the musty scent of moss and pine needles underfoot permeated the air. Then the trail broadened out and Rod dropped back to ride alongside the honey-blond wisp of a girl with the Mona Lisa smile upon her face.

"Tell me about Mt. Desert, Rod. Judging from some of the names I've seen I would say there had been a French influence in its history as well as English," observed Nicki.

"As a matter of fact, this island was named by the explorer Champlain, when he landed here in 1604. A few years later French Jesuits established a mission but it was quickly dispersed by the English. The first English settlement came in the mid-1700s," he expounded. "Just on the other side of this belt of pines in one of the island's most magnificent estates, 'Frenchman's Court.' I've never been inside. The owner is rather reclusive whenever he's in residence, but I've heard that it's full of priceless objects from all over the world. He's rumored to be a multimillionaire collector."

"Sounds more like a museum than a home," laughed the girl. "Give me a cozy cottage any day, they can keep their big drafty mansions!"

"Well, I wouldn't exactly call Frenchman's Court a 'drafty mansion' from what I gather," remarked Rod. "The original house was destroyed in the big fire of 1947. The current structure is barely ten years old."

"You can move right along now," urged David Trumbull as he came up beside them. "I think that's enough history for one day." Nicki chuckled at the theatrical annoyance in his demeanor.

"Relax, my friend," Rod teased him. "I've got my own girl, I'm not out to steal yours—though she's mighty tempting."

"Hey, you two, behave yourselves," scolded Nicki lightly, knowing full well that their banter was done entirely in fun. She gave Zephyr a slight urge forward, going ahead of the two young men to join Jenny Stewart.

"Enjoying yourself?" Jenny smiled warmly.

"Uh-huh. Zephyr is a dream. I can't thank you enough."

"I-I hope you'll come over to Oceanside and ride her any time you'd like. I mean that, Nicki!"

"Perhaps I will. I used to love to ride. I'd forgotten how marvelous it can be."

"Nicki—I don't usually intrude on other people's lives, but it's about David. I-I think he's developing quite a case for you. Dave and I have been friends for a long time and I wouldn't want to see him get hurt."

"Oh, Jenny, I'm sorry to hear that. I told David there can never be anything between us," Nicki said in a voice barely above a whisper. "He—he knows I'm in love with another man. David is very nice and I hope we can be friends, but that's all we could ever be to each other."

"I-I'm sorry I pried, Nicki. Please don't cry. I've brought up a painful subject for you. Forgive me."

"It's all right, Jenny. I thought I couldn't cry over him ever again, but I guess I was wrong. I have to get over it sometime—I may as well start now. Maybe if I talk about it, it won't hurt so much," Nicki sniffed.

"I understand, honestly I do!" insisted the other girl fervently. "I-I'm in love myself . . . only the guy doesn't know it. He's never given the slightest indication he wants to be anything more than a friend to me."

"Oh . . . Jenny."

"I was hoping you were luckier than I've been. Does 'he' know how you feel about him?"

"I-I made him believe it was just a passing physical attraction. He thinks I hate him! There were so many complications, Jenny. We won't be seeing each other again."

"Oh, Nicki, how can we both be so unhappy in love?"

"Let's talk about something else, before we get all melancholy and weepy and spoil our beautiful afternoon," urged the young Englishwoman as she stuck out her small dimpled chin. "What are you wearing to your party Saturday night? That seems like a good safe topic!"

"Well, if you really want to know I bought a new sundress. It's a peach color with straps that tie at the shoulders with a coordinating shawl. It's long but not terribly formal," she answered, wiping away a tear with the back of her hand. "What about you?"

"I only brought a few long things with me so I guess it will have to be the lavender silk skirt with the ivory blouse. I-I've only worn it once since I've been in the States."

"Ha! Here Rod and I figured you two were exchanging deep dark secrets by the looks of it, and what do we find you discussing . . . clothes! That's women for you, Rod," teased David as he and his friend caught up with the two girls. "Come on—we'll race you to that giant pine up ahead!"

It was a night of midnight-blue summer skies, crystal-clear stars beyond count, and a thick slice of moon high above. A cool breeze came off the water to waft through the treetops as if their limbs were nature's windchimes. Nicki was dressed and waiting on the front stoop when David Trumbull drove up in front of his brother's house. He eased himself from behind the wheel and sauntered up the walk. The girl was nearly hidden in the shadows yet he knew she was there by the sweet fragrance of her perfume and the vague outline of her figure against the clapboard house.

"There she waits—the mysterious lady of the night— and all I can see is her crowning glory, her laurel of spun-gold hair," he murmured. "I'd like to take her into my arms and show her that I make love like a man, not a boy. Would she hate me if I tried, I wonder? Or would she perhaps find herself falling in love just a little bit with me?" His breath came rapidly.

"You know the answer, David. I-I couldn't use you that way. T-to try to forget another man."

"You're so beautiful, Nicki, and I want you so badly that I almost wouldn't care if you did." He came up close behind her. Pushing aside her mass of thick blond hair, he pressed his lips to the side of her neck.

"Please . . ." Her voice was hoarse. "You're only making it harder for both of us. I-I don't *want* to love him, David. Don't you understand—I wish I did love you! We can't choose who we love, more's the pity. I know what it feels like to be hurt. I don't want to do that to you!"

"You can't stop hurting me any more than you can stop loving him, Nicki. What is his name anyway? It seems impersonal not knowing at least the first name of the man I hate without ever having met him." Bitterness filled his voice.

"Eric . . . let's just say 'Eric,' " she muttered. "Please try not to be bitter, David. Can't we be friends, good friends?" Her tears flowed fresh.

"Don't, Nicki—God, I'm sorry, honey. It's a beautiful summer night and we're going to eat and dance and laugh and forget all about love and hurt and bitterness. We're going to be just two people out together to have some fun, with no complications. Okay?"

She shook her head in agreement, not trusting herself to speak.

"Why don't you run along back upstairs and fix your makeup. I'll go honor my dear brother and his spouse with my presence for a few minutes." He flashed her an encouraging smile.

Nicki scooted back into the house and up the steps to her room. She pressed a cold compress to her red-rimmed eyes and splotchy cheeks, followed by a light application of eye shadow and mascara. Fixing a gay expression upon her features, she descended to rejoin her escort.

"This is Oceanside!" The girl's gay laughter floated on the night breeze. "From the way dear Jenny spoke of it I envisioned a modest summer cottage, not a three-story mansion." Nicki stood looking up at the gabled, English Tudor edifice surrounded by immaculate lawns and shrubs, its numerous windows ablaze with light. "It's magnificent!"

"But beneath that happy, confident mask that Jenny wears is just another 'poor little rich girl' who is afraid she won't be loved for herself, but her money," David said. "She'll inherit a bundle on her next birthday and I wouldn't be a bit surprised if the first thing she did was give it all away. At least then she could go to Rod and let him see that she's in love with him and she'd find out soon enough how he feels about her. I think he's crazy about her, myself, but the guy is proud and he'll never have the kind of money Jenny comes from. If she gives the money away Rod will know for sure that it doesn't matter to her. Then I wouldn't be surprised if our two friends tied the knot before the year's out."

"So—it was Rod she was talking about! Oh, I hope it all works out for them, David."

"They won't be able to say the same for you and me, will they, golden-girl?"

"David, you promised!"

"So I did. It's just that I'm crazy about you and I don't know what to do about it."

"I know the feeling."

"We're a fine pair of fools, my love. Come on . . . here we stand at the front door, let's go in and join the party. I can hear the band playing and at least while we're dancing I get to hold you in my arms."

"You're incorrigible, young Mr. Trumbull." She smiled at him fondly.

"Hey, are you two lovebirds going to stay out there all night or are you going to come in and join the crowd?" a gay voice called from the open door.

"We're coming—I was just pointing out the architectural wonders of Oceanside to this sweet young thing," David chuckled.

"Sure!" came a second voice. "Sounds like Trumbull to me," the voice said to its companion. "His lines are as ancient as the Parthenon, yet trite and unoriginal as they may be, they always seem to work for him. Beats me how he does it!"

"Hey, Nicki . . ." David's voice was low.

"It's all right, David. I wish you were just handing me a line." She slipped her arm through his in an empathetic gesture. "Isn't it about time for our big entrance, sir?"

"Good evening, miss, Mister David," greeted the formally attired butler with a slight inclination of his bald head. Nicki caught her breath as they entered the Stewarts' home, for the vestibule was dominated by a magnificent ornate chandelier. It lit up the marble-floored entrance hall like a thousand small suns.

"Good evening, Wadkins. Is Miss Jenny out in back?"

"Yes, sir. Everyone is out on the south patio, if you'd care to join them. If you'll excuse me now, one of the maids will take your drink order in a moment." He returned to his post.

"Good evening, miss, sir, what would you like to drink?" A black uniformed maid appeared as they proceeded toward the terrace.

"Champagne, for me, I think," Nicki supplied after a brief pause.

"I'll have scotch and water," added David. "It never ceases to amaze me, Nicki, but no matter where we go that woman will find us and she'll have the correct order. I guess the Stewarts can afford the best of everything. Well, we've put it off long enough, honey, here goes," and he guided her through the French doors and out onto the patio.

"There's David now! Darling—" A clear feminine voice rose above the chatter of the crowd as Nicki and David stepped outside once again. Nicki felt a blush rise to her face as several dozen heads turned in their direction at the sound of the woman's voice. This was no small get-together as the girl thought it would be—there had to be several hundred people milling about the large stone patio. Countless Oriental lanterns provided a soft glow to the surroundings. There were half a dozen gaily decorated tables filled with plates of hors d'oeuvres and tea sandwiches. A fountain of sparkling champagne flowed continuously and portable bars were scattered about. A dance band played under a canopy at one end of the terrace.

"Want to eat, drink, or dance?" asked David.

"Yes!"

"In that case, let's dance. They're playing 'our song'!"

"But we don't have a song."

"We do now!" And he whirled away with Nicki in his arms. "See how well we dance together, my love. That usually means something."

"It means we were both forced to attend dancing school," she laughed.

" 'Miss Aubrey's,' every Wednesday," he confessed with a broad grin.

" 'The Misses Christabel's.' " A giggle escaped.

"If they could only see us now."

"We do them credit." And they laughed together and moved among the other couples on the dance floor.

Nicki found herself enjoying the party immensely. She danced with David and Rod Charles and half a dozen handsome young men who all seemed to know one another. She consumed dozens of little delicacies made of water chestnuts and bacon, stuffed mushrooms, and spicy meatballs, all washed down with numerous glasses of bubbling pink champagne.

"It's a lovely party, Jenny. I don't know when I've had so much fun. I like your friends—they make me feel so gay!" Nicki stood talking to her friend while David and Rod went to refill their glasses.

"And they like you, too, Nicki. Especially the male half of the population. You look somehow different tonight—kind of radiant. Even in a crowd like this you stand out. Hey—maybe tonight you'll meet some tall, dark handsome stranger who will sweep you right off your feet!"

"Why, Jenny Stewart, don't tell me you're psychic! Do you have a crystal ball into which you peer to see the future?" giggled Nicki, not totally immune to the effects of four glasses of champagne.

"I wouldn't have thought so a moment ago," gulped her

hostess, "but there's a tall, dark, and very handsome stranger heading toward us at this very moment!"

"You're kidding," laughed Nicki as she twirled around to see the stranger Jenny had foretold.

Every semblance of color drained from the young woman's face, and her legs suddenly felt wobbly, as though they could no longer support her. Her heart was pounding in her ears. There was indeed a tall, handsome man making his way through the crowd, but this was no stranger—for the man was Eric Damon!

"You must be Miss Stewart," he stated politely, "my hostess." He smiled down at the red-haired girl standing before him, unleashing the full effect of his considerable charm upon her. And it was certainly not lost on Jenny Stewart. She smiled back at the man, never taking her eyes from his lean, dark face. "Please allow me to introduce myself. I am Eric Damon—a business associate of your father's and a close neighbor of yours. I am the owner of Frenchman's Court." His every word seemed to create an atmosphere of intimacy between the two of them.

"H-hello, Mr. Damon."

"Please call me Eric."

"Eric, then . . . and I'm Jenny."

"And this is . . ."

"Oh, excuse me, this is a friend of mine visiting us from England, Nicole Swithin," Jenny mumbled, embarrassed that she had been prompted to remember her manners. This man certainly had a devastating effect on the female senses.

"Miss Swithin," he repeated with a gleam in his blue eyes. He reached out for Nicki's hand and slowly brought it toward him. Then before she realized what he had in mind, Eric turned her hand over and pressed his lips to the pulse on the inside of her wrist. It was a wholly intimate gesture. Nicki jerked her hand away as if his touch burned her flesh.

"Oh—" Nicki inhaled and then held her breath. She simply stared at Eric, unbelieving and a little horrified. How? Why was Eric here? The question went around and around in her head.

"Your champagne, Nicki," came David's familiar voice at her side. "Hey, you look a little green around the gills, honey. Do you think you should drink anymore?" Nicki merely nodded and took the glass from his hand. Her own was trembling so that she was forced to steady the glass with both of her hands.

"Mr. Damon, I'd like you to meet David Trumbull and Rod Charles. This is our neighbor from Frenchman's Court—Mr. Eric Damon," said Jenny.

At the mention of the tall, dark stranger's Christian name, David Trumbull's face took on a contemplative scowl. He stared at the young Englishwoman as if seeking the answer to his unasked question in her pale face.

"Come on, Nicki, this is our dance," David finally said. But another hand came out to extract the champagne glass from her hand.

"She was just about to dance with me. You will excuse us." It was unquestionably an order that the tall, dark man issued, not a request. It brooked no argument. Eric took a firm grip on the girl's arm and unceremoniously propelled her ahead of him onto the dance floor. Nicki twisted and turned within his grasp, wincing at the pressure of his fingers on her arm. She glanced back for a moment at the small circle of astonished faces. Opening her mouth to offer some kind of explanation, she suddenly recognized the utter futility of words under the circumstances. She snapped her mouth shut again—her pale lips a pencil-thin line of despair. How could she make anyone understand.

She couldn't live without this man . . . yet could she bear to be with him?

Pulling her roughly into his arms, Eric brought her up tight against him. He gently forced Nicki's two small hands behind her back, easily grasping both of them within one of his own. His other hand came up to caress the silky nape of her neck in a curiously intimate gesture. Red-hot flashes of embarrassment shot through her body.

"Take your hands off me!" she hissed in his ear. "This isn't dancing—it's an insult! I can only guess at the perverted pleasure you must derive from subjecting me to this brand of degradation. Well, now that you've made it clear what kind of woman you think I am, let me go, Eric. Please—everyone is watching us." Her voice filled with the desperation she was feeling.

"Let them watch. I don't give a damn! You look very beautiful and very desirable. What man could keep his hands off of you? Every male on this dance floor wishes he were in my shoes, especially that hot-headed youngster being restrained on the sidelines by your friends. He must be a recent addition to your list of conquests," he said sardonically.

"Aren't you a little confused, Mr. Damon? I don't have a list of conquests, that's more in your line than mine," she replied sarcastically.

"Then who's the young Romeo? He looks like he'd enjoy nothing better than landing a hard right to my jaw."

"That's David," she said quietly. "H-he's been kind to me, Eric, when I needed someone to be kind. He knows there's someone else in my life. I told him right away that we could only be friends. I didn't lead him on. Please let me go now, I don't want any scenes."

"Someone else in your life," mused Eric softly. "What is the name of that young attorney back in England?"

"Mark—Mark Winstead?" she asked, perplexed at this sudden question.

"Yes, that's the name." His voice was strangely lazy and caressing. "But it doesn't matter, whenever I get close to you like this, I say to hell with the rest of the world. For a while it's only the two of us. All I can think about is holding you in my arms, tasting your lips, caressing your long swan-white neck and all the sweet secret places your body entices me with." His finger traced an imaginary line across her lips and down her neck to the hollow between her breasts. "I can't get you out of my mind. I want you, Nicki!" he whispered urgently.

"D-don't you dare say that to me!" Her eyes blazed bright green with anger. "I haven't forgotten the circumstances of our last meeting, even if you have, Mr. Eric Damon. You want me. Well, I don't want you! And what did you expect after I saw a half-naked woman stroll into your kitchen after spending the night in your apartment, and obviously in your bed as well! Supposedly your 'ex'-mistress, Nadine was certainly back in favor in short order. You don't even bother to get rid of the old before you bring on the new. Well, it makes my stomach turn. My flesh crawls to think you went from me t-to that woman. You disgust me!"

"Don't kid yourself, sweetheart. You tell me one thing, but your body will always betray you. You can wrap it up in as many pretty words as you think you need, it all comes down to one simple truth—you want me as much as I want you! I have always admired honesty above all else—and I imagined you to be the soul of integrity, Nicki, so don't disillusion me," he said through his teeth, his jaw set and hard.

"Don't disillusion *you*—now *that* is a good one." The sheer audacity of the man left Nicki trembling with rage, on the brink of tears. "Have you always been so cynical, Eric, or did your cynicism grow right alongside your ego? Have you never believed in anyone or anything other than yourself? Is anything so precious to you that you would give up your own life to preserve it? Is there nothing beneath that cold, unrelenting exterior but a twenty-dollar gold piece where your heart should be?"

"Have you quite finished?" Eric asked in a tightly controlled voice. "Perhaps once you've grown up a little, dear child, you'll learn to take people as you find them, to accept them as they are without trying to change them to fit your own standards. At least Nadine accepts me for exactly what I am. I don't explain myself to any woman, not even to you. I told you that morning in New York not to jump to conclusions, that things weren't the way they seemed. You can take that or leave it, Nicki. I will not be held accountable to anyone—do you understand that?"

"Oh, yes, Mr. Damon, you have made yourself perfectly clear on that point." Her laugh was harsh and slightly out of control. "You answer to no one . . . unlike other mortals."

"Oh, I'm mortal all right," he said with a twist of irony in his baritone voice. "In many ways I'm just like any other man—only perhaps less a fool than most because I don't delude myself about people. I acknowledge their few strengths and their many weaknesses, just as I recognize my own strengths and weaknesses. That's the big difference—I know what I am and why. And that's more than most men can claim."

She put her head back and looked up at Eric, studying the lean, patrician features, the dark handsome face, the penetrating blue eyes that could make her heart beat faster across the entire distance of a room. And it would always be that way, she supposed. Twenty years hence she would turn quickly at some large boring cocktail party and catch just a glimpse of a tall, dark-haired stranger and the memory of *this* man would flood every pore of her being. Oh, God, she thought, I can't bear it! If only her love for Eric was strong enough to sustain them both, because Nicki realized she was hopelessly and desperately in love with him. Whatever their future held, whatever the obstacles they would face, whatever the differences between them— this man was the great love of Nicki's life and she knew it with all of her heart! *We must not blame Eric for what he has become, Nicki. He is afraid to love us back.* That's what Louisa Olivetti had said to her. But the frustration was almost more than she could bear.

"If you continue to look at me like that, young woman, I won't be held responsible for my actions. I'd like to take you in my arms and abscond to my home with you, locking all the doors and windows!" Eric said in a gruff tone.

"I-I would probably let you if I thought you loved me," she whispered.

"Love is an illusion, Nicki. And I am above all a realist."

"So for you it's only physical desire. But desire can fade away when the dawn comes, leaving only spent passions and a bad taste in one's mouth. Perhaps you can face a future of going from one love affair to another, but I can't live that way, Eric. I believe in love and marriage with one man for all of my life!" She pleaded for his understanding.

"I know, Nicki, I know," he said tensely. "Why do you think I've kept away from you these past four weeks, working sixteen-hour days, exhausting mind and body so I would drop into bed each night to sleep like the dead? It was either that or come after you as soon as you left New York, probably to our mutual regret. I-I foolishly thought if I gave it a few months I'd stop thinking about you—you would become a pleasant interlude, a beautiful girl whose face though imprinted on my mind would fade with each day. I-I held out for a month, then I had to see you!"

"Oh, Eric, I wish I didn't love . . . I wish I'd never met you! There's no going back, no forgetfulness for me, not now, not ever. I think I could almost hate you for that. You've ruined me for any other man. I'll always compare him to you and find him wanting. It's not fair! Oh, God, I can't stand being near you—let me go!" she cried out, breaking his hold. She ran blindly, anywhere, to get away from this man and the terrible hurt she felt.

"Nicki . . ." Eric called after her, his voice thick with emotions even he did not understand. But she never heard him.

"Nicki . . ." This masculine voice was younger and kinder. "Are you all right?"

"Oh, David, is that you? Would you mind terribly taking me home . . . back to Clare's?"

"Sure, whatever you want. You look awfully white, kid."

"I-I have a splitting headache," and it was suddenly true.

"Come on then. I'll tell Jenny that we're leaving. Nicki —Damon's the guy, isn't he?"

"Yes, David, he is."

CHAPTER SIX

It was a gray, drizzly afternoon. Nicki stood aimlessly at the window looking out at the beach, staring at the rain-drenched dunes below the house and then beyond to the white-capped waves pounding unceasingly onto the shore. A shudder ran through her thin frame. Tugging at her sweater, she pulled it closer, wrapping her arms around herself. Each day of the past two weeks had taken on a merciful sameness, enabling her to walk through the motions of living without putting her heart into it. For Nicki's unexpected meeting with Eric Damon had left her already raw emotions exposed like a reopened flesh wound. She had retreated into herself as an act of self-survival. It had become a matter of self-preservation.

"But, oh, Eric—what am I going to do about loving you?" she whispered to the windowpane. You must avoid him at all costs, the practical side of her nature spoke up. The man was dangerous! For one thing, he makes you forget the very principles you've been brought up to believe in, the moral standards on which you have based your entire life. In less than a month now you'll be returning home to Cheswick, to your father, your lovely familiar house, and to Mark . . . dear, dependable Mark, who has loved you unfailingly nearly all of his life. Mark, who wants you to be his wife and the mother of his children.

Fool! Stupid foolish girl! Even you aren't that naive. How could you marry Mark now? This tall, black-haired man with eyes that can be as warm and inviting as a tropical sea or as wild and turbulent as a tropical storm . . . it's this man who brings you alive as no one else ever could. Without Eric's arms around you, without his kiss upon your mouth, you're only half-alive . . . only half a woman. Can you honestly deny that in your heart you know you'd rather be Eric's mistress for one night of grand passion than Mark's wife for the rest of your days? And if that's true then it would be horribly unfair to marry Mark even if you vowed never to see Eric again. From the moment Eric Damon first kissed you, you were his and his alone.

"Oh, God . . . I don't know," she moaned, her hands clutched to her breast in agitation. But she knew one thing for certain—she must sit down and write to Mark Winstead. It was the least she could do. And with that decision made, she grew calmer.

It was a sharp rap at the door of her bedroom that finally interrupted her musings.

And then there was a cheerful voice calling out to her. "Nicki, are you there?"

"Is that you, Jenny? Come in!" she called back, turning around just in time to catch a glimpse of a freckled grin peering around the corner.

"Doggone, it looks like our ride has been rained out again! 'Into each life some rain must fall, some days must be dark and dreary.' Wasn't it Longfellow who penned those immortal words? Now I should know who said that—after all, there must be something to show for the very expensive education I've received."

Nicki shrugged her shoulders and smiled, thinking how fond she had grown of Jenny Stewart in just a few short weeks.

"Say, you aren't up here in the garret pining away on a lousy day like this, are you?" Jenny flopped her boyish figure down on the bed, dangling her long legs over the edge. "Now I've put my foot in it," she mumbled as the color rose in her friend's face. "Ah, Nicki, hasn't he called you yet?"

"N-no, no, Eric hasn't called, not since the morning after your party. You know that I asked Clare to tell him I wasn't in, but I don't imagine for a minute that Eric believed her. I-I just couldn't talk to him then. Can you understand that, Jenny?" Her blue-green eyes, big and round and uncertain, posed the question too.

"I think I can, but the question is whether Eric Damon does. Do you want to see him, Nicki?"

"I-I don't know. Perhaps if he were to call again . . ."

"Look, Nicki, I'm going to be brutally honest with you because I like you a lot and because I like to see my friends happy. And it's obvious, at least to me, that you aren't happy. Eric Damon didn't strike me as the type of man who would ask a woman twice—any woman. He doesn't play by the same rules we do, it isn't even the same game. If you want to see him again you'll have to go to him!"

"I know that what you're saying is true, but I have my pride, Jenny. Eric and I simply don't have a future together. There's so much more than fifteen years separating us. He's a very wealthy man who has traveled the world, mixing with heads of state, the renowned, the jet set, the titled. I had never been out of England until this summer. My father and I live in a comfortable home, but it's not large and by some standards I suppose a little shabby. I don't mean that I'm ashamed of my home or my way of life—if anything, just the opposite. I just don't think I could function in Eric's world."

"There are snobs and superficial, shallow people in every economic class, Nicki. The wealthy are no different than the poor, in that respect. And with a man like Eric—he would be your world."

"I know, but that's not the whole problem. I-I have to be able to live with myself. I have to retain some self-respect. Eric isn't the marrying kind—he's made that implicitly clear. I can't have him thinking I'm chasing after him the way so many women do."

"In other words, he won't marry you, but he wouldn't object to having an affair, is that it?"

"Yes—don't you see I would just be one more name on his list? A list that I'm sure includes some of the world's most beautiful, sophisticated, and wealthy women. I wouldn't even be special to him, just a pretty young thing whose name and face he would forget all too soon. But—I would remember every detail about him, about every moment we'd ever spent together until the day I die. I couldn't stand that, Jenny. I couldn't stand not meaning anything to him."

"You must love him very much."

"I do!"

"Then don't underestimate yourself, my friend. You're beautiful and you will still be beautiful when you're eighty. You have talent and intelligence and you love him. I say you can hold your own against his jet-set girl friends any day!"

"Oh, Jenny, you are a dear."

"Hey, Nicki, surely you don't plan to just pack up and go back to England without seeing him at least one more time? I-I wonder what he would have said to you if you'd taken his call. I mean after all you were the one who wouldn't talk to him. Just don't let pride alone rule your actions—you have to live with your regrets for the rest of your life."

"I know." Her voice was a whisper.

"My car's parked right outside and I won't need it for the rest of the afternoon. Perhaps you'd like to take it for a drive. A breath of fresh air would do you a world of good."

"Perhaps I will."

"Here's the keys," Jenny said, extracting a keychain from her jeans. "And, Nicki—just follow the main road to Shoreline Drive. Frenchman's Court is the second drive on the left."

"Thanks . . . for everything!"

Five minutes later Nicki found herself behind the wheel of Jenny's sleek red sportscar speeding along the main road, reassuring herself that a long, leisurely drive would definitely lift her dampened spirits. She had not a single intention of showing up uninvited at Frenchman's Court. If Eric wanted to see her he would just have to call again. She was simply out for a drive and drive she did.

Farther on down the coastline, she noticed that as the trees and underbrush thinned out, the shoreline gained a rugged, austere appearance. One dark wave after another smashed itself up against the black, algae-covered boulders, blowing its spray upward into the sky to mingle with the rain before they plummeted to the earth together.

It took Nicki back to other gray rainy days on another coast—the west coast of England. She had gone there as a young girl to Gaby's cottage, frequently visiting for the weekend with her parents. She had felt an affinity for rainy days even then.

The cloud-covered sky would give way to a light, steady drizzle. Nicki would pull on her mackintosh, grab a battered umbrella from the vestibule closet, and make her escape. She always chose the same well-worn path down to the shore, tapping the metal tip of her "walking stick" on the wet stones, chuckling under her breath, "Elementary, my dear Watson, elementary." Thick patches of fog hovered here and there. Baker Street fog—and she, she was a snug sleuth under her cape. Indeed, she was Sherlock Holmes, strolling along the beach, lost in thought over his latest case.

"And where is the little girl you once were, Nicki?" she asked herself out loud, the tears pricking at the back of her eyes. "The world was a simpler place then," she gently reminded herself. Dreams came true in childhood fantasies. You simply closed your eyes and you could be whoever or whatever you desired. You were limited only by your imagination. You could even be the greatest fictional detective ever created, if you wanted to be. Life had been warm and wonderful and secure, with a loving mother and father. Life never hurt you then. Until one day a careless lorry driver had snuffed out the life of Abigail Swithin as she stopped her bicycle by the side of the road. No one knew why she had stopped—it could easily have been to catch a glimpse of a rare breed of wood thrush in a nearby thicket. That was the kind of woman she had been. But with the loss of her mother, Nicki grew up. For a long while the young girl never smiled and she never pretended to be Sherlock Holmes ever again. Nicki firmly put her childhood behind her at the tender age of eleven. Then gradually as the months passed the hurt became a numbness and with the resilience of the young she learned to smile again.

It's not going to be any easier this time around, she told herself. To cut Eric out of her life now was to cut out her very heart. For all her protestations, Nicki knew she would rather be fighting tooth and nail with Eric than making love with any other man. And when he held her in his arms and kissed her all that mattered was that he should never stop.

Nicki swung the sportscar around in a sharp U-turn and raced back up the coast road she had just traversed. She had no difficulty in following Jenny Stewart's instructions and within a few short minutes she could discern the mammoth steel gates of Frenchman's Court. That they were locked seemed obvious by all the electronic gadgetry. Then she spied a small metal box recessed into one side of the gate. She pulled off the road and with purposeful strides went right up to the box and opened it. She gingerly picked up the telephone receiver inside and put it to her ear.

After several moments a refined male voice spoke. "Good afternoon. For security reasons would you please state your name."

"Uh . . . this is Nicki, Nicole Swithin, but . . ."

"Welcome to Frenchman's Court, Miss Swithin. You may proceed up to the main house now."

"But I don't understand—do you know who I am?" She could not resist asking the question.

"I beg your pardon, miss, but Mr. Damon gave instructions that if you were ever to come to Frenchman's Court or any of Mr. Damon's residences you were to be admitted immediately. I'll open the gates now, miss."

"Th-thank you." Slowly replacing the telephone receiver she closed the metal box before returning to Jenny's automobile. She waited with a sense of rising anticipation as the gates majestically swung open in front of her. She drove through the steel jaws of Frenchman's Court and watched them close in the rearview mirror.

Nicki made her way up the winding drive, noting to herself that most of the land had apparently been left in its natural state. There were no formal gardens here nor carefully tended flower beds, but acres of tall straight pines, prickly brush, and small scampering wildlife. And then the house came into view and Nicki was pleasantly surprised for the second time in as many minutes. For this was no cold monstrosity as she had imagined, but a simple Dutch colonial house—the outside finished in a pale yellow siding. The double pitch of the gambrel roof presented a soft profile against the sky, and a covered porch ran the full length along the front of the house. At least from the outside it seemed to be a warm, inviting, old-fashioned home. Admittedly it was a great deal larger than most, but all the same, a home.

Leaving her automobile parked in the drive, Nicki nervously made her way along the flagstone path that led up to the spacious front porch. Almost at the touch of her hand on the brass knocker, the door was opened by a pleasant-looking woman of perhaps fifty, her iron-gray hair braided and coiled and then secured to the crown of her head in a rather dated style.

"It's Miss Swithin, isn't it? Won't you come in? I'm Thula Berman, Mr. Damon's housekeeper. Let me take your raincoat and umbrella."

"Thank you," the girl responded.

"This way, miss," the woman indicated with a smile and a flourish, as she guided Nicki across the threshold of Eric's home into an entranceway of bright yellow walls and red brick floors. She could see ahead to a delicately curving staircase with newel posts, balusters, and banisters of rich dark cherrywood. A dramatic chimney dominated the living room beyond as it rose to meet the ceiling a full two stories above. Glass-fronted bookcases flanked each side of the fireplace, and two red-velvet wing chairs were grouped with a rose-and-gold brocade couch.

"This is lovely," said Nicki in an appreciative tone. "It seems cozy, although that's not a word I would usually apply to a room of this size. Perhaps it's the generous use of wood paneling. I-It's so different from the New York apartment— Oh, excuse me, Mrs. Berman, could you tell Mr. Damon that I'd like to see him?"

"I would be happy to if I could, Miss Swithin, but I'm afraid Mr. Damon has been called away on business. He left nearly two weeks ago. Pardon me for saying so, but I am surprised he didn't inform you of his departure. I believe he meant to. But it was one of those emergencies that a man in his position cannot avoid. He only had an hour's notice."

"An hour's notice," she parroted. So that's why he hadn't called again. It explained so much. "Actually, Eric did call my cousin's house, but I wasn't in and he left no message." It was the only explanation she could offer this woman. "When do you expect him back, Mrs. Berman?"

"We never know, Miss Swithin. Sometimes it's a week or two, sometimes it's several months."

"Oh—" The dismay Nicki felt was clearly reflected on her face.

"But we were all told by Mr. Damon to make you feel at home in his absence. He thought perhaps you might like to come here to practice your music. The piano is directly behind you. And we have a guest room prepared if for any reason you should decide you'd like to stay here at

Frenchman's Court. Mr. Damon wished for you to consider this as your home while he is away."

"Th-that was most generous," said Nicki a little uncertainly as she sauntered over to the grand piano, running her fingers over its shiny keys. "What a superb instrument. It looks brand new."

"It is, miss. It was brought in just before Mr. Damon left on his business trip. To my knowledge, no one has ever played it."

The young woman felt her cheeks grow hot at the implication. Could it really be that Eric had had a piano installed in his home just for her pleasure? How did he know she would ever be inside Frenchman's Court, for that matter? The thought was curiously disturbing. Or . . . or was the piano a form of bribery? What other man could tempt her on such a grand scale? No—no, he needed no other bribes when it came to women. No, it wasn't that, she realized. Eric was attraction enough.

"It's nearly four o'clock, miss—would you care to join me for a cup of tea and perhaps some cream cakes? That is, if you don't think it inappropriate for me to ask? I baked the cakes fresh this morning just in case Mr. Damon returned unexpectedly. They're his favorite."

"I wish I could, Mrs. Berman, but I borrowed a friend's car to get here and I have to return it this afternoon. So, unfortunately, I must decline your kind offer."

"Well, I'm sure there will be many other times, Miss Swithin. Please come visit us at your convenience and I'll tell Mr. Damon that you were by to see him the moment he returns."

"Thank you, Mrs. Berman." But as she drove away she muttered softly to herself, "I only hope it's not too late, Eric."

* * *

It was nearly dusk. Nicki and Jenny had finished packing the large wicker picnic hamper. The silverware and napkins had been double-checked and they were finally ready to leave for the cookout.

"Did you stick those two old blankets in the trunk of my car, Nicki?"

"Yes, sir, captain!"

"Hm—by the time we get to the beach the lobster and clams should just about be ready to eat. There's a lot more to a roast like this than meets the eye."

"I know Rod and David and the other guys have been working all afternoon."

"Yes, it's quite a process, but the results are delicious. First, they have to dig a pit in the sand and prepare a thick bed of hot coals in the bottom. Then it's a matter of layering the lobster and clams alternating with layers of seaweed. And it looks like we've got a perfect evening for a cookout, too. Well, we're ready to go. I'll take the basket —would you grab my guitar there behind you?"

"I've got it," Nicki answered as she picked up the black leather case and followed her friend out to the car.

It was only minutes later that Jenny pulled her sportscar in between half a dozen others on a small bluff above the beach.

"From the looks of the crowd down there we may be the last to arrive—again!" teased the redhead as she pointed to perhaps a dozen young people scurrying around the pit.

"So—you finally decided to come," called David as he spotted the two girls struggling down the beach, arms piled high. "We were going to go ahead without you, but it seems you've got all the silverware!"

"Well, of course," giggled Jenny. "I planned this gala

evening and I made certain that the necessities were assigned to Nicki and myself. We have, in addition to the silverware, the napkins, plates, butter, salt, and pepper. I made sure you couldn't start the party without us!"

"Now that we *are* here, let's dig in! I haven't had even the tiniest morsel since breakfast," Nicki supplied. "My dear friend here made me promise I would starve myself in preparation for this feast."

"In that case, come, my love—you will be number one in the chow line—a much-coveted position at these affairs, so I understand," said David with an exaggerated bow. "Here is your equipment—plate, knife, fork, nutcracker, pick . . ."

"Wait a minute, wait a minute. What in the world do I need all of this for?"

"You may not be aware of this, milady, but tonight you will be working for your supper. Unfortunately, for man, the lobster does not jump out of his shell for our eating convenience."

"And I'm so hungry," moaned Nicki.

But two hours later she had changed her tune. "Oh—no more for me, David. It's delicious, but I couldn't eat another bite!"

"My, my, what a finicky appetite," he said aside to Jenny and Rod. "She's just consumed two entire lobsters *and* a dozen clams and she wonders why she feels so stuffed?"

"Don't forget I fasted nearly all day," she reminded him, pursing her lips into a slight pout, tracing circles in the sand with her finger. They looked from one to another and then burst out in contagious merry laughter.

"Play something for us, Jenny," a girl suggested from the other side of the campfire.

"All right, but why don't all of you sing along," she

suggested. Her graceful, agile hands moved on the strings of her guitar in an opening chord. "Let's start with 'Barbara Allen.'" And they all joined in the singing of the familiar ballad.

'Twas in the merry month of May,
When green buds all were swellin',
Sweet William on his deathbed lay
for the love of Barbara Allen.

They sang verse after verse, their shiny faces visible above the red-orange light of the flickering campfire. They sang sad songs and silly songs, ballads and gay rollicking tunes. They ran the gamut from the "Tennessee Waltz" to "Where Have All the Flowers Gone?" They sang until they thought they could sing no more.

"Oh, come on," urged Nicki, her face aglow. "I feel as if I could sing all night."

"Sing for us then and I'll follow along," Jenny encouraged her friend. And the others added their pleas to Jenny's.

So in the still of that night, with the waves gently lapping at the shore, with the moon a glowing orb overhead, and Jenny softly strumming her guitar, a clear sweet voice sang out.

Black, black, black is the color of my true love's hair.
His lips are something wond'rous fair
The purest eyes and the bravest hands,
I love the ground whereon he stands.
Black, black, black is the color of my true love's hair.
I love my love and well he knows,
I love the ground whereon he goes

And if my love no more I see,
My life would quickly fade away.
Black, black, black is the color of my true love's hair.

The last note died away. One young man silently rose
to his feet and poked the dying embers of the fire with a
stick. Then someone finally cleared his throat and suddenly everyone was talking at once. And it was only then
that Nicki realized that the wetness on her face was her
own tears. She quietly turned away to erase what evidence
she could of their existence. Whatever had possessed her
to sing that particular song, she wondered. Had she been
subconsciously thinking of Eric yet again? Was she never
to escape the folly of her own traitorous emotions? Without Eric would her life quickly fade away? She was all too
afraid that the words of the song could prove to be true
for her.

"That was beautiful, Nicki." It was David coming to sit
beside her on the blanket. "My luck—I would have to be
a blond . . ." He let the irony of the situation speak for
itself. "I'll be leaving Bar Harbor in a week to return to
the university. I understand you'll be leaving soon, too."

"Y-yes, I fly to London at the end of next week, in fact.
I've missed seeing you lately, David." Her head was bent,
her voice low.

"I take it this doesn't represent a change of heart on
your part—as in 'absence makes the heart grow fonder'?"

"Not the way you mean, I'm afraid. But I'd hoped we
could be friends."

"You make it very difficult for me, Nicki. You know
that I'm in love with you and I know there's no future in
that. The less I see of you right now the better off I'll be
when you're really gone. I just couldn't be the platonic
friend you wanted, that's all there is to it."

124

"Is it that bad, David? I'm sorry I . . . ." But whatever the girl had been about to say was buried under an avalanche of sound quickly descending from the bluffs above. The shrill notes of several whistles, the excited barking of a dog, the thud of boots hitting the sand, all heralded the imminent arrival of two uniformed policemen.

"Good evening, officer," Rod ventured as the two men approached the campfire.

The first man nodded. "I'm Officer Henderson and this is Officer Simmons. I'm afraid we're going to have to break up your party—this is private property, which makes all of you guilty of trespassing at the moment."

"Trespassing!" repeated Jenny. "But I've used this strip of beach before and never had any trouble."

"Sorry, miss, but this is definitely private property and we have to ask you to leave."

"Golly, I wonder if someone complained, or what," she said to Nicki. "Well, we were about to pack up and go home anyway, I guess."

But Nicki did not hear her, for all of her attention was focused on a shadow beyond the fire. She peered into the darkness surrounding the figure, but could not make out a single detail. It was only the sudden racing of her pulse that revealed to her and her alone the newcomer's identity before he moved closer.

"Good evening, officer," a deep, strong, authoritative voice said from outside the circle. "Any trouble here?"

"Who in the devil . . . ?"

Then the man behind the voice stepped closer to the firelight and everyone, including Nicki, was looking up into the devilishly handsome features of Eric Damon!

"Mr. Damon," gulped the officer. "I didn't realize it was you, sir."

"That's all right, officer. What seems to be the trouble?"

"We were just taking care of this matter, sir. We'll have these trespassers off your property immediately."

Nicki let out an audible gasp at the imparting of this information.

"I'm afraid there has been some kind of mistake made —these people are my guests, not trespassers." And his tone of voice left no doubt in the policeman's mind that this man wanted the matter dropped.

"Yes, sir. Come on, Simmons. You'll excuse us then." And the two uniformed men retreated with their dog in tow.

"Thank you, Mr. Damon." Jenny was the first one to regain her poise. "We didn't mean to cause any trouble, honestly. I never thought about this part of the beach as belonging to Frenchman's Court."

"That's all right, Miss Stewart," Eric smiled. "I don't think you'll be bothered anymore tonight, but perhaps the party should be considered 'finis.'" Eric allowed his gaze to touch each one of them in turn before it came to rest on Nicki and David, whose arm was casually draped across her shoulders. "Yes, the party's over!" There was a certain grimness to the set of his mouth now. His eyes caught Nicki's over the fading light of the fire—neither spoke aloud but she felt her name on his lips.

"Let's pack up and move out!" Rod's voice carried across the night. He stood up and brushed the sand from his denims. Then, looking down at Jenny, he held out his hand and pulled her up beside him. "Come on, honey, I'll take you home." And the girl smiled back at him with stars in her eyes.

Frenzied activity ensued as the young men and women gathered up their picnic baskets and shook the sand from their blankets before they began to drift in groups of three or four back to their automobiles.

Nicki rose slowly to her feet and nearly stumbled as she discovered her legs felt as if they were made of jelly. Eric stepped forward and put out a hand to steady her.

"You're coming with me." He wasn't asking Nicki, he was telling her.

"Why should she go with you?" David moved toward them.

"Because Nicki belongs to me—and she knows it."

"I don't 'belong' to any man!"

"You heard the lady, Damon. Come on, Nicki." David made as if to turn and follow his friends.

Eric stared hard down into her face and she felt the undisputable force of his will. The look in his blue eyes both frightened her and excited her to the very marrow of her bones. She felt as if she were precariously balanced on the edge of a precipice—she could either pull back now to safety or plunge ahead into the uncertainty Eric offered.

"Nicki? David? Aren't you coming?" Jenny's voice came from farther up the beach.

"Nicki?" David's question came one last time.

"I—I'm sorry, David."

He looked from the young blond creature—ignoring the eyes that asked for his understanding—to the dark triumphant figure of the older man.

"I hope you know what you're doing." Then he turned and left to join the others waiting for him.

Eric studied her pale face for a moment before he spoke. His words startled her. "If you run you can catch up with your young friends. It's still not too late to change your mind, Nicki."

"It was too late a long time ago," she whispered.

CHAPTER SEVEN

After the others had gone, they stood there side by side for a moment on the darkened beach—the slender young woman in the faded jeans looking out at the sea, the tall, broad-shouldered man beside her, mute and motionless. A thick curtain of clouds drifted in to cover the moon. The last flicker of the fire died away, leaving only the ashy remnants, before the silence was broken.

"It sure is dark out here." She meant it as a casual comment, but it came out sounding like little more than a child's unspoken fear of the night.

"Surely you aren't frightened, are you?" He reached out for her hands, holding them between his own. "Nicki, your skin is like ice! Why didn't you tell me you were cold?" She shook her head, but he had already turned, drawing her along with him as he headed away from the beach. He wasn't giving her a chance to think, Nicki told herself. And if she quit thinking she would be lost. She dug in her heels, balking at his touch.

Eric stopped dead in his tracks. "Aren't you coming with me after all?"

"W-where are you going?" she asked inanely.

"Didn't your mother teach you not to answer a question with a question, young lady?"

"Did yours?" she threw back at him, shamefully aware that her retort had struck the target.

"That hit was below the belt." His tone was deceptively gentle.

"We're awfully good at hurting one another, aren't we, Eric?"

"It would seem so."

"Is this the way to Frenchman's Court?"

"Yes, a shortcut between the main house and the beach. It's a five-minute walk from here." He softly hummed a tune as they made their way along the path. Then he pulled up and spoke next to her ear. "Is black the color of *your* true love's hair, little one?"

"Hrrmph, don't patronize me, Eric Damon! It—it was just a song. I've always been rather partial to blonds, I think." She made her voice go dreamy.

"Really." But she sensed somehow that he had not cared for her answer. "I rather think I prefer dark hair myself."

"Yes, but today's brunette is tomorrow's blonde at the touch of a chemical."

"And you, golden-haired girl, did you get that glorious head of hair out of a bottle?"

"Actually, it's none of your business, but no—it just so happens that this is my natural shade."

"Then you're all *you* from your golden head to your pink toes." The way he said it made the blood rush to her face. He did know, of course. Apparently he had not forgotten that night in New York any more than she had.

Every time he had touched her a strange thrill had shot through her body, making her weak with desire for him. She loved this man and she wanted him and he wanted her. It was an explosive combination.

Hands stuffed into the pockets of his fitted black trousers, Eric slowed his pace to a leisurely stroll. Through the trees ahead Nicki could see the dark looming hulk of the house.

"Mrs. Berman told me you had been up to the house in my absence." He put it out as a feeler, placing it before her as if they were opponents finally meeting at the peace table.

"Y-yes, I-I was out for a drive one day and thought I would stop to see—the house. I'd heard so much about Frenchman's Court."

"And how did you like my home?"

"It wasn't at all what I expected. It's quite the loveliest house I've seen. I think it was a case of love at first sight for me, but then who wouldn't love this house? I expect you've heard that from everyone." She was completely honest with him, at least when it came to her feelings about his home. "But why did you name it Frenchman's Court, Eric?"

"I didn't, it stayed on from the previous owner. It seems there was some speculation that the island's first settlement was on this site."

"Oh, Rod Charles told me that the first settlers were French Jesuits—hence, Frenchman's Court."

"Something like that."

"H-how long have you been back?" She finally mustered up the courage to ask the question uppermost in her mind.

Eric glanced down at his watch, depressing a small

130

button that lit up the dial. "Exactly two hours and seventeen minutes."

"Oh, and did you take care of the emergency then?"

"Yes."

"And now . . ."

"Now I sit back and relax. I never do business in this house. There are no stacks of papers here, no briefcases and secretaries, and only two people have the telephone number. I will only take the direst emergency calls and they both know that. I do not entertain business associates here. In fact, other than Mrs. Berman, Wadkins, and the security man you are the only other person who has been inside my home in the ten years since I built it!"

Nicki held her breath, hardly daring even to breathe. "You mean that Nadine and all the others—not a one has ever been in your house here?" It seemed so incredulous.

"You are the first 'friend'—male or female—that I have ever allowed inside my home. I come to Maine to relax, Nicki, to walk through my woods or along the beach, to swim in the nude off a private cove. This is my sanctuary. I want no associations here with my life in the outside world. Here I can be what I like. I wear shabby jeans and don't shave for a week at a time, I can sleep until noon or stay up all night with a good thriller. There are no timetables or schedules here, no ticker tape, no television—although I think Mrs. Berman has a small one in her apartment over the garage—no photographers, no reporters. Here I have privacy!" He spoke with such conviction that Nicki necessarily looked up to study the lean, handsome features she knew so well. Her heart missed a beat or two when they came within the sphere of light coming from the back porch, as she saw for the first time how tired and haggard Eric looked.

"You look exhausted," she commented, wishing with

131

all of her might that she had the nerve to reach up and soothe the crease from his brow. "Perhaps you should spend more time at Frenchman's Court and less in the world outside, as you put it. I don't know how you can bear to leave this place, anyway."

"It's not quite so hard to leave it in the winter, although that has a beauty all its own here," he said to her. "It gets very cold here, Nicki."

"That's not what I meant. You need a long rest, Eric, you've been pushing yourself too hard."

"I have just come from three weeks of conferences and negotiations that would have sent most men straight into the hospital. I am still standing on my own two feet. But you're right—I plan to spend more and more time here and at a beautiful little villa in the south of France that I've just purchased. I am gradually turning over my business interests to others. By the time I'm forty I will be retired for all practical purposes. I may do a little lecturing, perhaps write a book, but that will be it. There's no sense in having money if you don't have the time to enjoy it."

Nicki bit her lip, clamping down hard to keep herself from crying out. Oh, Eric, she thought to herself, it could be so perfect for us if only you would let it. Surely in the life you have planned for yourself a loving wife and perhaps eventually children could be a part of it. But she kept quiet, for Nicki realized that Eric had just allowed her to get closer to him than perhaps anyone in his life, that she had been allowed to see a side to him that few people even knew existed. She dared not press that trust.

"Here we are." He took her elbow and guided her through a backdoor and down a hallway, where he flicked a switch and the lights came on. Blinking several times at the sudden brightness, Nicki opened her eyes to discover she was standing in the center of the kitchen. It was a big country-style kitchen with the same split-brick paving on the floor as she had admired in the front entrance, and with an old-time butcher block in the middle. "Would you like something to eat?" Eric asked her as he opened the refrigerator and studied its contents for a moment. "Mrs. Berman usually leaves me a midnight snack around here somewhere."

"There's a note on the counter," offered Nicki.

"Ah. 'Mr. Damon: sandwiches and homemade soup in the fridge. Put in microwave oven for two minutes. Mrs. B.' Care to join me?"

"I don't think I could, Eric. I ate so much earlier tonight—well, perhaps one sandwich and a little soup," she conceded as she saw the deep scowl on his face and realized that he was not in the mood to eat alone.

"Fine. You'll find the soup mugs in the cupboard behind you." His countenance had brightened once again.

Is this how it would be? Nicki asked herself. The two of us coming back from a late stroll on the beach, warming our supper together, and then carrying it on trays upstairs to the library? It was a smaller, cozier room, a distinctly masculine domain with bookcases lining the walls and overstuffed leather furniture, and a gas fire flickering in the grate. An intimate room with the aroma of briarwood permeating the air. Nicki's eyes alighted upon an elaborate wood rack of carved pipes. She had not even known that Eric smoked a pipe. How much more was there to this man that she did not know? The possibilities seemed to be endless.

"I-I didn't see this room when I was here before. Of course, I wasn't upstairs at all." Nicki made small talk as Eric cleared a place on his desk for their trays and pulled up a second chair. "This room suits you and this house."

She was handed a mug of steaming chowder, which she sipped while watching Eric out of the corner of her eye. He was devouring a third sandwich in between gulps of hot soup and Nicki could not help but wonder how he kept from burning his mouth. Why, he acted as if he were a starving man eating his first meal in days!

With his attention fully on his meal, Nicki indulged herself, letting her eyes linger on each sharply chiseled feature of his handsome face. Even with the hint of dark circles under his eyes and a whitened pallor, Eric was still the best-looking man she had ever seen. Her gaze slid down the length of his body, flooding her with memories of the feel of his sinewy form against hers. Just the thought of this man made a shiver of delight pass through her body. Her hazel eyes filled with the sweet torment she felt whenever she was near Eric but not within the circle of his arms.

"Nicki . . . Nicki, would you like some coffee?"

"Huh . . . oh, yes, thank you" was all she could manage. Eric gathered up both trays and left the room. The young woman moved closer to the fireplace, nestling herself in one corner of the long leather couch.

"Th-this is coffee?" she burst out in surprise at the crystal mug of dark brown liquid topped with whipped cream that Eric placed in her hands several minutes later.

"Take a sip."

"Hm, it's delicious," she reported contentedly as she took yet another sip. "What is it?"

"Keoke."

"Keoke?"

"Coffee dressed up with crème de cacao, coffee liqueur, and a float of brandy—and of course, topped with plenty of rich whipped cream."

"Keoke—well, I like it!" she sighed as she put her head back and closed her eyes. "It's very peaceful here."

When she opened her eyes again she knew instinctively that she was being watched. She turned to find Eric's deep blue eyes delving into her own with a sleepy sensuality.

"Eric." He took the coffee cup from her hands and set it down on a nearby lamp table.

"Now it's my turn," he mumbled as he stretched out on the couch, pulling her down beside him. As soon as he had her comfortably settled, her head cozily snug against his chest, one of her arms across the hard muscles of his abdomen where he clasped it in his own, he closed his eyes and was instantly asleep.

Well, this is one fine predicament you're in, Nicki, my girl, she said to herself. You can't even move to scratch a twitchy nose or see your wristwatch without waking him up—and the nerve of the man. Why, he knew it! This was simply Eric's way of insuring that she didn't have second thoughts about being here with him, that she didn't slip away into the night while he caught a much-needed nap!

Nicki took several deep breaths, willing herself to relax since there was little else she could do under the circumstances, but the heat of Eric's body so close to her own and the scent of his cologne in her nostrils only set her on pins and needles. Relax, she snorted to herself, *that* was a laugh! Well, just count the swirls in the ceiling, she told herself then. The absurdity of her situation hit the young woman between forty-nine and fifty—the young lithe body shook with muffled merriment. Here she was, lying in this man's embrace in the most intimate of settings and she was staring at the ceiling, counting the swirls in the plaster! Despite her determined efforts and the sharp little teeth she sunk into her lower lip, the suppressed laughter rocked through her body.

Then she froze—the laughter dying in her throat. For Eric seemed to partially rouse from his sleep. Shifting his body first one way and then the other until one heavy leg was thrown across both of Nicki's, his face turned to nuzzle her throat. His warm breath ruffled the collar of her shirt. The girl glanced down and nearly gasped, for his movement had somehow twisted her shirt until the top buttons had come undone. The lacy edge of her bra was visible and she was very much afraid that from his present vantage point if Eric happened to open his eyes that wasn't all he could see!

She grew rigid as if suddenly aware of the intimacy Eric suggested in his sleep. Nicki couldn't take much more of this, that much was certain. The tension in the air was thick enough to cut with a knife.

As if her subconscious thoughts had been relayed to the sleeping form beside her, Eric's eyes began to blink open. Nicki could actually feel his eyelashes fluttering against the bare column of her throat. The blood pounded in her head as she felt the soft touch of his lips on the spot where only a moment ago his long lashes had teased her into awareness.

Eric groaned her name as he lifted two heavy, sultry eyes to hers. Then his mouth swooped down to take hers in a searing kiss that touched her very soul. Nicki made a strangling sound beneath him, pressing her hands to the broad expanse of his chest as if to push him away. But Eric was relentless in his attack on her senses until he felt the girl give herself up to the wild torrent of passion that burst anew between them, her hands curling into the hair at the base of his skull.

He pressed her down farther and farther into the leather couch until she cried out in pain against his lips as the buttons of her shirt jabbed into her ribs. He pulled back, but refused to release her mouth as his kiss took on a different texture. Now it became tender and gentle as if he were drinking from a cool, dark pool, quenching his thirst for her with long, soothing drafts. A strong hand caressed her shoulder and then her shirt where her breast rapidly rose and fell, her heart fluttering like a captive bird's, and then slowly to her waist where the soft white skin lay revealed to his touch.

With one finger he drew ever-enlarging circles on the girl's bare abdomen, setting her aquiver from head to toe. And then as quickly as he had begun, Eric bolted upright, nearly tottering Nicki to the floor. With a single urgent motion he jerked the black sweater he was wearing over his head, carelessly throwing it to the floor. In the glow of the firelight, his tanned muscular chest glistened like that of a golden Adonis. As if mesmerized by the sight Nicki reached out to touch the perfection of Eric's body as it hovered above hers. At her touch, a tremor shook the big man. In a voice quavering with desire he half-commanded, half-begged the girl to touch him. Her inhibitions unleashed, Nicki allowed herself to explore every inch of Eric's back and chest—but when he would have drawn her hands lower, she instantly recoiled in fear. He let it pass, not pressuring the lovely creature beneath him, all too aware that she was not ready to do as he would have bid her.

Eric lowered his face again to hers, kissing her with all the charm and innocence of a schoolboy, easing her fears until they melted away. As the man felt her relax in his arms, his mouth searched deeper into hers and she met him eagerly with her own. A wildfire burst aflame, bringing them once more to the point of excitement where only the total union of their bodies could ease the ache they felt for each other. Eric's hand rested on her thigh and this time it was the man who would have moved to caress her as no man had ever done. But Nicki was suddenly aware that her belt buckle had been unhooked and the zipper of her jeans partially undone. Eric bent his dark head, pressing his searing lips to the white softness beneath her breasts.

"No! No!" She heard her own cry as if it came to her from across the long distance of a dream. She struggled upward, as if to consciousness, her arms wildly flaying at him. Her heart was like a heavy hammer thudding against her breast. "No! I can't, I just can't!" And she lay there trembling, racked with dry sobs that wrenched the very soul of the man from his body.

"Oh, Nicki," he moaned in self-depreciation. "It's all right now, my darling. Everything will be all right." He repeated it again and again in a gentle tone, passion quickly fading from his troubled eyes as he rained soft kisses on her eyelids and face and the tiny tips of her ears. He held her then as one would hold a child to still their fears. "Damn! I forget how very young and sweet and innocent you are!"

Nicki was finally able to choke out the words of explanation to the man beside her. "Oh, Eric, I-I want you and I know I've been a disappointment to you, but I just couldn't do it! I don't know how to be a mistress—I don't know how to be with a man! I tried, but I just can't do it!"

"It doesn't matter, Nicki, honestly it doesn't," and there was a look in his eyes that Nicki had never seen there before. "First we're going to sit up and then I'm going to get us two strong brandies while you put yourself to rights." His voice was calm and Eric was once more in total control of himself. "Then we'll just sit and talk and when you're feeling calmer I'll take you home to your cousin's."

"Yes, Eric."

When he returned to the library five minutes later, Nicki was sitting on the edge of a large leather chair, her hands folded primly in her lap, the only remaining evidence of their embrace the heightened color of her cheeks and the rumpled state of her hair. Eric thoughtfully handed her a comb without comment and once she had rectified the tousled masses of honey-blond hair he eased a brandy snifter of amber-colored liquid into her hands. Then he took his own drink and went to a seat opposite her, a safe distance away.

He was once again clad in the black V-necked sweater that had been so carelessly shed only minutes earlier. Placing his arms on his knees, Eric grasped the glass between his hands and leaned forward. "I can't say that I'm sorry for what happened between us, Nicki. I've never seen myself as a hypocrite. You're a desirable and lovely young woman and there's always been this spark between us. It was bound to happen, you know that as well as I do."

"I know, Eric. I'm not asking anyone for apologies."

He leaned back in the chair, his long granite legs stretched out in front of him. He studied her clear, direct gaze for a moment before expelling a hard breath as if he had needed that reassurance from her. Then he went on. "I, uh, talked with Madame Olivetti this afternoon before I flew out of New York. She asked me to give you her love." A puzzled frown settled on his brow. "You two certainly became fast friends considering I only took you to see her twice while you were in New York." He paused and then looked up straight into her eyes as if he expected to find the answer to his question there.

"I did visit Louisa one other time on my own." Nicki suddenly felt as if she were walking a tightrope.

"Is that when you started calling her 'Louisa'?" His voice had a razor-sharp edge to it.

"Yes, I suppose so." She tried to sound noncommittal.

"What did you and Louisa talk about?" He was trying to be as nonchalant as she had been, but Nicki spotted a vein pulsing wildly on his neck. She didn't understand what he was up to but she recognized that it was dangerous ground she was treading on.

"Well, I'm not sure I can remember anything specific. After all it's been some time now. I suppose we chatted about our music and how I was enjoying my trip to New York . . ." The girl's face was tinged vivid pink, as she squirmed uncomfortably in her chair. It was as if she were a laboratory specimen put under the microscope for examination.

"Just normal, polite conversation between two acquaintances then?" he asked pointedly.

"Yes."

"And on the basis of that 'normal, polite conversation' you now call Madame Olivetti by her Christian name? A proud, reticent, dignified lady who could give lessons to a duchess, a woman old enough to be your grandmother? And she—she sends you her love?"

"Are you jealous? How long was it before she allowed you to call her Louisa?"

"That is entirely beside the point." There was a ruddiness to his cheekbones that had not been there before. "You know, Louisa lectured me about you." He switched his tactics.

"How awful for you," she said dryly.

"Yes, well, I'll admit she was subtle about it, never even mentioning you by name. But I suspected what she was up to from the beginning."

"What she was up to?"

"To spell it out for you, my dear sweet child, Louisa Olivetti was matchmaking."

"Matchmaking!"

"Must you repeat everything I say? Yes, you heard me correctly, she was matchmaking between you and me, Nicki."

"Are you sure?"

"Of course, I'm sure."

She felt a low chuckle start down in her throat. "Considering how gun-shy you are, I wouldn't be surprised if you thought you saw a scheming female behind every bush."

"I wouldn't exactly put Louisa in the 'scheming female' category!" She flushed, sensing his sudden irritation with her.

"I didn't mean it like that and you know it!" she said, her sense of humor fleeing. "You don't have to go out of your way to make me feel like a gauche schoolgirl!"

"If the shoe fits, wear it!"

"Well, of all the insulting . . ." she sputtered, jumping up.

"Sit down, Nicki." Then he put the question straight to her. "Did you and Louisa talk about me?"

"Of all the conceited, big-headed . . ."

"Did you?"

"I don't know. I suppose your name may have come up in passing."

"In passing, huh? You were always a poor liar, my dear," he said, making it clear he did not believe her. "You confided in Louisa, didn't you, Nicki? Did you tell her that you're in love with me? That I came close to seducing you, nearly compromising your fine English sense of honor?"

"Of course not!" she raged back at him. "I-I wouldn't tell her something like that."

"Like what? Like you love me?"

"Yes . . . no . . . oh, sometimes I think I hate you, Eric Damon!"

"So—you did tell her that you're in love with me!" Her face was in flames now, her only thought to escape his cruel interrogation. "Yes, I can just see it now." A twisted smile of satisfaction curled his mouth. "Did you two plot together, going over every detail as to the best way to bring me to rein?"

"What?"

"Matrimony, my dear girl, we're talking about matrimony!"

"That's a despicable thing to say, Eric."

"Is it?"

"Yes, I've never asked anything of you at any time during our—our . . ."

"Relationship?"

"Relationship. I have never once mentioned marriage to you, as well you know. As a matter of fact, I would never marry you."

"Why not?" He seemed surprised at her vehemency.

"First of all, you're simply not my type. I don't happen to like handsome men who think they're the answer to every woman's prayers. Well, you're certainly not the answer to mine. Have you forgotten already, my dear man, you're not the marrying kind? And in my opinion, which I'm sure doesn't mean a fig to you, it's a good thing you aren't. I don't think you'd make a good husband. And in my book that's no compliment. You make no commitments to any woman, that's what you declare as if it were something to be proud of, as if it were a banner to be waved in front of you. Well, it's adolescent."

"Adolescent!"

"Yes. A mature man regards marriage as a union between himself and a woman who is his equal. Not as a trap that some conniving female lays to catch him as if he were some kind of prize to be won at the fair. Marriage isn't one-sided. The man doesn't lose his freedom while the woman gains everything. It's wanting to be together because you love each other. But as you say, you make no commitments to any woman—not to a wife, not to a mother. Well, I wouldn't brag about it. I think it's pathetic, that's what I think!" She broke off, choking over her own words.

Eric's eyebrows were lifted high into his forehead and for once Nicki had the satisfaction of seeing the color drain from his face.

"What made you say that?" He was suddenly as taut as a panther crouched in the high grass waiting for a chance to strike its victim.

"Say what?" She dared him to look at her.

"What made you say that I make no commitments, not to a wife or to a mother?"

"I don't know, perhaps because it's true. Now will you please stop shouting at me. I can't think straight when you yell in my ear."

"All I want from you is a straight answer." He grew quiet again, but the uncompromising tone was still there in his voice. "Look, Nicki, you've made it very clear what kind of man you *think* I am, and you're welcome to have your own opinion. But there are things about myself that I haven't told you and perhaps it's time I did." He sighed, then got up, moving to open a black lacquered box on his desk. He withdrew a cheroot and lit it, inhaling several times before he continued. "I think I told you once that I grew up in an orphanage until I ran away finally at fourteen. Oh, Granville wasn't any worse than any state-supported institution, I guess, but it was understaffed and overcrowded and from a very young age I knew the meaning of the word—illegitimate."

Nicki cringed at the word he had left unspoken between them.

"I'm not asking for your pity, Nicki!"

"And you're not getting it!" she cried out. "But the little boy you were a long time ago—surely I can feel something for him?"

Eric stared down at the girl for long moments before he went on with his story. "Anyway, I ran away, determined to someday make a great deal of money for myself, so much money that no one could ever tell me what to do, ever again. For a while I washed dishes in a greasy backstreet diner in lower Manhattan and peddled newspapers on the street corners, and I even had a shoeshine stand. Until one afternoon when I was down by the docks I saw a Greek freighter and decided to see more of the world. I jumped a cargo ship and sailed for Greece the next week. She was halfway across the Atlantic before they discovered their extra passenger. Or I should say crew member, because I was put to work swabbing the decks for the remainder of the crossing."

Eric smiled, his gaze turned inward. "I was bold as brass at fourteen, with a chip on my shoulder that I literally dared the world to knock off. It cost me more than one black eye along the way. But I was a hard worker and I knew how to use the brains God gave me. I was down on the pier fishing one morning when I met a boy of my own age. We talked and fished and as the weeks passed became good friends. One day Andros took me home to meet his parents and the next thing I knew they gave me a room of my own right there in their home. Eventually, I discovered that Andros's father was the Greek shipper whose vessel I had stowed away on in the first place. They were

144

good to me, Nicki. Andros was the best friend I ever had. We finished school together and then we started to learn the ropes of the trade side by side. But at eighteen, Andros was paralyzed in an automobile accident and he died six months later. His father had no other sons, no one to turn to, so I stayed on alone and learned the shipping business. I was paid very handsomely, treated like the son they had lost. And it was about that time I discovered a natural ability when it came to investing money. I studied, of course, but somehow I knew when it was right to buy and when to sell. By the age of twenty-one I had more than made my first million."

Nicki sat as if glued to her chair, her attention never wavering for a minute.

"About twelve years ago I was approached by Granville to endow their scholarship program for bright youngsters —something like 'graduate makes good'—only as I remember it they discreetly asked that I not mention how I came to leave their hallowed halls. Money opens many doors that are shut to a kid with no name, Nicki. I read my own file on one visit to Granville. That's how I found out that my mother was told I had died at birth. I located a retired doctor who had been an intern at the hospital and he was able to fill in the rest of the story for me. It seems that the head resident at that time felt that the stigma of having an illegitimate child would ruin my mother's career and her life. She was quite well known in her field, and I suppose in those days it would have. And there was some question about her own chances for survival at the time. But between my money and my attorney, I eventually found my mother."

"You found your mother!" Nicki was dumbfounded by his statement. "You know who your mother is! Have you ever told her that you're alive, that you're her son?"

"No. I thought about it for nearly a year, Nicki, and in the end I decided that it would be more than she could handle. I was twenty-five years old—a grown man. How do you walk up to a stranger and tell her that you're the son she thought dead at birth? No, I just couldn't do it. So I did the next best thing—I arranged to meet her at a party one night in New York and I made friends with my own mother." He paused for a moment and then took a deep breath. "Perhaps you'll understand better if I tell you that Louisa Olivetti is my mother, Nicki."

The tears flowed unheeded down the young woman's face. So she was finally to hear the other half of this story. To think that all these years this man and his mother had each endured the agony of knowing the truth without being able to share it with the other. Each unselfishly thought to spare the other the pain. How difficult it must have been for Louisa to look upon a face so much like her own lost love and not call him "son." And now they had both confided their past to her. It was almost more than Nicki could bear. She was the only one who knew—the only one!

"Hey, I wouldn't have told you if I'd thought it was going to upset you like this. You're crying as if your heart were breaking. What is it, Nicki?"

"I-I kne . . ."

Eric suddenly grew thoughtful. "It didn't surprise you, that's it! You already knew that Louisa is my mother, didn't you, Nicki?"

"Yes," she whispered, inwardly begging for the older woman's forgiveness.

Eric sat down, wearily, pressing his hands against the fine black hair of his head. "I assume Louisa told you herself." He glanced at Nicki for confirmation. "So she's known all along."

"About the same time you have."

"And she never told me."

"Just as you never told her."

"I think I'll have another brandy. This night is turning out to be more than I bargained for."

"What are you going to do, now that you know?" Nicki had to ask him.

He stood by the window for a moment, a great shadow of a man. And Nicki suddenly had a vision of a tired and lonely Eric Damon. She would have gone to him, comforted him, but the formidable front he presented to the world would have frightened even the strongest of heart. He was proud and arrogant and he would not welcome the knowledge that Nicki also knew he was lonely.

"Nothing, I will do nothing. Louisa has her reasons for keeping silent all these years. I will respect those reasons."

"B-but Eric, what if she kept it to herself because she was afraid to risk losing your friendship? What if she thought you might end up hating her? It wasn't out of shame that Louisa kept her secret!"

"Are you sure, Nicki? Because it's very important that I know for sure."

"I'm certain. In the beginning Louisa wouldn't come forward because she felt she had no right to. You had just become a wealthy man. She was frightened that you would reject her, thinking she had only now acknowledged you because of your money. She had her pride, too, and she'd been on her own for so many years."

"Did she tell you the whole story?"

"Yes, she did."

"I suddenly feel as though you know more about me than I do myself," he said with a shake of his head.

"That's not true, Eric, not really. But I can't say any more. It's your mother's story to tell, not mine. I-I promised her it would be our secret—I hope that under the circumstances she'll forgive me."

"I'm going to see her, Nicki. We've both kept silent too long. Without you we may have never known. Tomorrow morning I'm flying back to New York. Now, come on, darling, it's very late and we've had quite a night. I think it's time I took you home."

Eric had driven her back to Nash and Clare's that night leaving her with a sweet promise of a kiss and the feel of his arms about her. Nicki thought of it again and again as first one day and then another and then another passed. He had told her he would be back in three days and she had lived for his call. But over a week had gone by now and Nicki was packing to return home to England. She knew in her heart that Eric wasn't coming back for her, that she had been waiting for a call that was never going to come.

"You have only yourself to blame, Nicki," she lectured herself as she folded the last blouse and put it in her suitcase. "Will you never learn when it comes to Eric Damon? Let's face it—you wanted to give him all of your love and the man just wasn't interested in your terms. He never said he loved you. He never encouraged you even the slightest bit into thinking it was anything more than a strong physical attraction on his part. He never made even one promise to you. You're a fool, a fool with a broken heart and it's your own fault! Why, he hadn't even been interested enough to find out when you had to return to England. You made a fool of yourself over the man again!"

Nicki snapped the last case shut with a definitive click and heaved it over the side of the bed to stand with the others on the floor. She looked around the antique-filled bedroom for a moment and knew she would remember this place always.

At least it eased the ache in her heart just a little to think that Jenny and Rod might find their happiness. Jenny Stewart had popped by the house earlier that day to say good-bye, her red-freckled face wet with tears of joy as well as sadness. She had confided to Nicki that her unrequited love for Rod Charles wasn't quite as unrequited as she had thought. He had been acting in the strangest manner lately, not at all like a brother or a pal, but more like a lover. And then she had hugged her blond English friend and made a dash for the door before her tears took over again.

Clare and Nash drove her to the airport that same morning, promising to visit their English cousin the next summer. They had wished her a safe journey home and then Clare had whispered, "Best wishes with your young attorney. I hope you'll be as happy as Nash and I have been." And Nicki had seen no good reason to go into an explanation in the middle of the airport terminal and so she had let it go by. She would write Clare a letter once she was home and straighten it all out, never dreaming that her decision nearly changed the course of her life.

CHAPTER EIGHT

It was a sun-bright autumn day, a day of golden hues and crisp country air. A brisk wind scolded the trees, picking at the soft curls of the young woman as she scurried along the path, a bundle of letters clasped in her hand. She burst in the side door of the cottage, shivering at the chill that nipped at her gloveless hands and the tip of her small pink nose. She hung her coat in the hall, then sailed along to the kitchen dropping the cache of letters and bills on the table before beginning the daily ritual of preparing tea. The kettle was put on the stove and a freshly baked pound cake sliced, thick creamery butter laid out with sweet sticky pecan tarts. With the table laid, there were several minutes remaining to sort through the post before Dr. Swithin's brisk walk would be heard coming from his office.

With the gracefulness of a feline, Nicki pushed the short honey-colored curls from her cheek and slid into a kitchen chair. Her shirtwaist dress was a beautifully cut silk creation with a soft swirl of scarf at the neck that emphasized her model-thinness. Her legs were encased in sheer stockings, her face expertly made-up. For this Nicole Swithin was chic, smart, from the short cap of fashionable curls to the expensive pumps gracing her petite feet. It seemed on first sight that she had never looked better in her life, but on closer inspection the small telltale signs were visible to the astute observer—a certain tilt to the chin, a hardness in the usually warm, friendly eyes, a distinct coolness in the voice. Where Nicki had once been open for anyone to read, now she was closed to everyone, even her father.

One pursuit dominated Nicki's life now: her music, almost to the exclusion of all else. She spent hour after hour, day after day, at the piano, perfecting her repertoire. Her style possessed a hard brilliance that had been missing before. There were plans for the young woman to join her godmother, Gabriella Fontini, in Paris the next spring. Together they would put the finishing touches on Nicki's performance before her debut the following September. Nicki was no longer a little girl playing at life, but a woman with a goal. She had made her decision—to dedicate herself to a career. Men no longer interested her.

Nicki quickly shuffled through the mail, glancing at each envelope in turn. She neatly stacked those addressed to her father by his place. There were three for her—a short, cryptic note from Gaby, an effusive detailed narrative from Jenny Stewart, and an airy one-page scrawl from her cousin Clare. Nicki read Clare's letter last. She read it once, then twice, staring at the sheet of thin airmail stationery as if she dared not believe the words she read. Even then it took several minutes for their impact to be fully realized by the young woman.

For Clare Trumbull casually mentioned that a tall, handsome man had come to the house asking for Nicki the very next day after her departure. Clare had informed him that her young English cousin had returned home. When he questioned her if it could really be true, she had reassured him it was; Nicki had flown home to England and was to be married. The man had seemed shocked and left without further comment. Clare had meant to tell Nicki of the incident in an earlier letter, but it had simply slipped her mind. She certainly hoped her omission had not caused any complications for her cousin since word had since been received that Nicki was not going to marry Mark Winstead after all. Clare chatted on for several more lines before closing with her apologies and love.

Nicki refolded the slim piece of paper and slid it back into its envelope, her movements absentminded, mechanical; her composure, carefully constructed over the long weeks, nearly slipping. So—Eric had come back, but too late, too late! It didn't matter anymore. If Eric had felt any love for her, if there had been any plans to include her in his future, where had he been all these weeks? Why had he not come to her? Where was he now? Surely the thought that Nicki was to marry another wouldn't be considered an obstacle by a man like Eric Damon. His lack of scruples when it came to his own wants and desires was nearly legendary. No—she was very much afraid that in his opinion she was simply the one who got away. In fact, Nicki should no doubt be thankful that Eric had delayed his return to Bar Harbor. For she knew that any further contact with him could only have led to more heartache for her. Evidently, she had done a first-rate job of convincing Eric that he was not her type, that she would never dream of marrying him. Yes, she had made that clear to the man and it was true, of course.

"Well, wasn't it?" she demanded of herself. "Aren't you lucky you got away before you'd committed yourself body and soul to the man? Yes, how fortunate you have been,

Nicki!" A harsh throaty laugh gave way to a torrent of tears. Tears that had been stored up inside her all those long weeks and months. Nicki finally put her head down on her arms and released all the anger and frustration and longing she had struggled to contain since her return to Cheswick.

"Nicki—my darling girl, whatever is the matter?" It was the compassionate, concerned voice of John Swithin that patients and friends alike had been responding to for a quarter of a century. He had quietly let himself in the back door for his tea only to find his daughter weeping as though she would never cease. It affected him deeply to see his only child like this—she had never been a girl prone to hysterics. And since the loss of his dear Abigail ten years ago, his daughter had become even more precious to John Swithin. It had been difficult at times to raise a young girl by himself, but he and Nicki had always been close companions, at least until the last few months. Dr. Swithin had thought for the past year or so that Nicki and Mark Winstead would be coming to him with the announcement of their engagement, but it had never materialized. Mark was now about to marry another girl after what amounted to a whirlwind courtship. The man had been surprised by how calmly Nicki had seemed to accept this turn of events, although he had never kidded himself that his daughter had been madly in love with Mark Winstead. Yet John Swithin did know that Nicki had been very fond of the young barrister and given time perhaps she would have fallen in love with him, as Mark had apparently been with her. That was all changed now and the doctor wondered if the realization that she did love Mark had come too late to his daughter.

"Is it Mark?" he prodded gently, placing a reassuring hand on her trembling shoulders. Then the man raised the young woman onto her feet, encircling her with strong, comforting arms. Nicki laid her head on the secure solidarity of her father's chest and shook her head no. So, it wasn't Mark Winstead causing this upheaval in his daughter's life. But then what or who was? The real change in Nicki had been apparent after her trip to the United States. The more he considered this bit of information the clearer it became to John Swithin. He tried again. "Is it a man you met in the States?" This time Nicki awarded her father with the answer he sought as she mumbled a teary yes. "I'll make us that cup of tea now, my dear, and if you would want to talk about it, I'm ready to listen and help if I can." He pressed a clean handkerchief into her hand and then went about the business of preparing their tea. Within several minutes, Dr. Swithin was placing a cup of strong dark tea onto the table in front of his daughter, before settling down on the opposite side with his own.

Nicki sipped at the hot liquid for several minutes before she finally chose to speak. "I guess you've noticed that I haven't been myself lately," she sighed.

"Well . . ."

"It's all right, Dad, you don't have to answer that. I know it's true and you haven't uttered one word of criticism. You've been so understanding. I-I just couldn't talk about it before, I guess it still hurt too much." Her small hand reached out for his in a gesture the old Nicki had often made.

"You've grown up, my dear. I don't expect the woman to confide in me the way the little girl did. You've become an adult, it's only natural you should want more privacy. I wouldn't really want it any other way. But that doesn't stop me from worrying about you, from recognizing that you're unhappy."

"Oh, Dad, I'm sorry. Here I thought I was hiding it so well, and while you've been worrying, I've been selfishly indulging myself."

"Don't be too hard on yourself, that's just part of being a parent. It goes with the territory as you will no doubt find out for yourself one day." John Swithin smiled at her affectionately.

"I don't think I'll ever have the chance to find out," she stated with a hint of drama. "I will never marry now."

"Nicki, Nicki, so skeptical and not yet twenty-one?"

"I-I met a man in New York, Dad. But there are problems, problems that I just can't see any solution to. There's nothing you can do."

"I can listen." Nicki's eyes brimmed with tears as she looked at the familiar, loving face across the table from her.

"Oh, Dad, I don't know what to do! I-I'm in love with a man named Eric Damon, but marriage just isn't in his vocabulary. Eric came right out and told me he would never marry."

"Some young men are afraid of marriage, Nicki. Perhaps as Eric matures he'll change his way of thinking."

"It's not a question of maturity, in this case. He isn't a young man, Dad. Eric is thirty-six years old."

"For some men the revelation that they want to marry comes with finding the right woman."

"I've thought of that, too. Maybe I'm just not the right woman for Eric. I've wondered if I would measure up in a world like his—he's a wealthy financier, a millionaire, in fact, a world traveler, a member of the jet set. He has four or five residences on both sides of the Atlantic. He even has a place in London. Eric drives expensive cars and wears only the best clothes. I don't know, Dad, perhaps I wouldn't fit into his world."

"My dear daughter, you would measure up in any world! And while all of that is interesting, what of the man himself? It's the man you must look at, not the accoutrements of his wealth."

"I know you're right, Dad. Eric's money doesn't attract me. In fact, just the opposite—I find myself put off by it. I've tried to see beyond the fancy cars and luxurious furnishings to the real man. But it's not easy. He guards himself well."

"He has no doubt had to."

"His mother said very much the same thing to me. Eric's proud and arrogant and brilliant, but I believe he's lonely too, and skeptical, that he needs someone who loves him in spite of all his material possessions. He spent his childhood without the love and security of a family. Eric is very much a self-made man. I doubt if he has ever acknowledged the need for anyone. But I think he would be kind and gentle, generous and loving with the right person. Someone who would teach him to share himself, no more, no less." She spoke in a quiet, thoughtful voice.

"And you'd rather like to be that person, but you have some doubts—could you handle it?"

"Yes. Although there were times when Eric was different with me, almost as if he were a little uncertain of himself. When I look back on it, it seems downright silly. I can't imagine Eric being uncertain about anything."

"Every man—and woman—has his Achilles heel, my dear daughter."

"Well, I couldn't imagine what Eric Damon's would be."

But John Swithin could imagine as he gazed at the lovely creature across the table. She was a beauty, this daughter of his and Abigail's, so much like her mother had been at the first flush of womanhood—young and tender, yet strong-willed, full of life, possessing a naturally sharp wit. A man could build his entire world around a special woman, but it made him vulnerable. For if anything should go wrong that world would crumble about his very feet. Once a man had loved and been loved by a woman like that all the others seemed second rate. He knew—it had happened to him. "Are you quite sure that it's love, Nicki, and not merely infatuation or physical attraction?"

"Oh, I won't deny the physical attraction that is there, but I also love Eric as I never dreamt I would love anyone. I can't seem to get him out of my mind no matter what I do. Oh, Daddy, I'm so afraid it's going to be like that for the rest of my life and I don't think I could bear it!"

John Swithin gave his daughter a chance to collect herself. "My dear, I wish I had the ability to keep the pain and hurt from your life, but I don't. Sometimes the hardest part of being a parent is the helplessness one feels."

"I feel a little helpless myself right now. I received a letter from Clare Trumbull this afternoon. She wrote that Eric came looking for me the day after I left Bar Harbor. She told him I had gone home to be married. Eric thinks I'm married to Mark Winstead!"

"I don't suppose you have done anything to correct that impression."

"How could I? Eric and I haven't exactly kept in touch over the months. Oh, Dad, don't you see—Eric never said he loved me. I couldn't just show up and yell 'Surprise! I'm still eligible!' He could easily throw it right back in my face. I won't beg Eric to love me. I will not subject myself to that kind of humiliation!"

"How proud we mortals are."

"It's all I have left. I won't forfeit my pride as well."

"But didn't you tell me what a proud man Eric Damon

is?" Nicki nodded her head. "And do you think he'll put aside his pride and come to you now?"

"No, no, I don't. I can't see Eric chasing after any woman. It's hardly his style. Besides, we had a little disagreement the last time we saw each other. I said some pretty terrible things to him. I swore I could never marry a man like Eric, that he was definitely not my type."

"Did he believe you?"

"I'm sure he did. I almost believed it myself."

"Almost?"

"Oh, Dad, when I'm with Eric nothing else really matters. I almost believe we could be happy together."

"Love is not just an outer attraction, but an inner magnetism that draws a man and a woman together, sometimes in spite of themselves. It means accepting the whole man, Nicki. Can you do that with Eric Damon? Someone like Eric has been forced to create a shell around himself for survival. But inside, where it counts, he, too, can be vulnerable, unsure of himself, sensitive to rejection. The male ego is often such a delicate thing. I believe it is entirely possible that you've trampled on Eric's," Dr. Swithin offered to his daughter.

"You mean I've hurt his masculine pride, that he thinks I've rejected him?" The idea seemed incredulous to the young woman.

"I'm simply saying that it's a possibility."

"Then there's no hope for us. Eric won't come to me and I won't go to him." All life faded from her eyes. "I just wish to God I didn't love him so much!" And her father heard the desperation in Nicki's voice.

When he returned to his office for the evening appointments, John Swithin sat at his desk for a few minutes, brows furrowed deep in thought. Then he suddenly became animated, excited, as if a difficult decision had been weighed and made. Quickly taking pen in hand he jotted a short note and stuffed it into an envelope. Two telephone calls later he had the information he needed. Scrawling an address on the front he put the envelope out for the post. It was with an extra cheerful smile on his face that Dr. Swithin came forth to greet his next patient.

It was nearly a week later that the doctor announced his plans. "I'm going up to London in the morning, my dear. I have some business to take care of, very boring for you, I'm afraid. I'll be gone several days—would you like me to ask Beth McGrady to spend the nights here with you?"

"That won't be necessary, Dad," replied Nicki with a puzzled air. "I'm a big girl now. I'll be all right here by myself." It all seemed a little odd to the young woman. Her father usually extended an invitation to her to accompany him on these occasional jaunts to London. But for some reason she felt that he preferred to go alone this time. Being her father was only one part of his life, she rationalized. He had a perfect right to go to London without her. He had his own living to do. "I hope you have a good trip, Dad."

"So do I, so do I!" stated John Swithin emphatically.

It was nearly one o'clock when Dr. John Swithin, dressed in his best three-piece gray suit and looking rather dapper, strolled into the lobby of one of London's finest restaurants. Its four walls bespoke of quiet elegance, privacy, discreet affluence. He stood for a moment in the red-carpeted, crystal-chandeliered lobby savoring its atmosphere like the bouquet of a good wine. Then he stepped forward, speaking briefly with the maître d', before he was escorted to a prime corner table. He ordered a glass of sherry and sat back to enjoy the quiet luxury that surrounded him.

Some minutes later a tall, dark-haired man, a man whose very posture suggested power and arrogance, entered the restaurant. The normally blasé maître d' scurried up to him, speaking in excited tones frequently punctuated with head-bowing and a flourish of hands. The scene was observed with avid interest by John Swithin. Then the man extricated himself from the small circle of people and walked across the expanse of the room toward the doctor. Every eye was on the approaching stranger, although he seemed unaware of the attention centered on himself. The man already seated was forced to admit that Eric Damon was devilishly handsome, that there was a magnetism about him that left neither man nor woman unaffected.

"Doctor Swithin?" He inclined his head slightly, reaching out to shake the older gentleman's hand.

"Yes."

"I'm Eric Damon."

"It was good of you to join me. Shall we sit down?" The two men stood facing each other for a moment, sizing up the opposition, as it were. Then they both moved to sit at the same time, the activity relieving some of the awkwardness of their initial meeting.

"What will you have to drink?" inquired John Swithin.

"Chivas Regal on the rocks," Eric said to the waiter.

"I'll have another sherry," he ordered for himself. Then Dr. Swithin leaned back in his chair and nonchalantly studied the other man. He had seen too much of life and death, of the rich and poor equally humbled by illness to allow even a man of Eric Damon's stature to ruffle him. But he could imagine the ice-cold fear that a single stare from those steel-blue eyes could instill in people. Eyes that spoke of a razor-sharp mind and a tongue to match. And to think that his little girl had pitted herself against this man—she had more guts than even he had imagined. Yes,

160

Nicki had her hands full with this one. "I understand you keep a home here in London."

"An apartment actually. I'm frequently here on business so it's a feasible alternative to hotels."

"And you're here this trip at the Secretary's invitation."

"You seem well informed for a country doctor. Yes, it's true, I've been asked to serve as a consultant at a series of economic conferences. I have government meetings on my schedule in various parts of western Europe over the next few weeks."

"Sounds interesting, but I'm afraid the world of high finance is a mystery to me."

"Just as your work amazes me, Doctor Swithin. A man at the top of his class at the medical college settling in a small village, choosing to be a general practitioner rather than a highly paid specialist."

"Ah-hum, I see you've done your homework, Damon. I never was ambitious when it came to making a lot of money. I had nothing to prove to myself or the world." He looked up at the younger man. "We've always been comfortable and that was enough for Abigail and my, uh, family." John Swithin hesitated, not yet ready to mention his daughter and thereby precipitate a conversation he preferred to bring up in his own way and in his own good time. "I had my own ideas about combining mental health and preventive medicine. My country practice has permitted me the time to try out some of those ideas and write a few pamphlets on my observations."

"You are too modest—six highly respected dissertations in your field could hardly be classified as 'a few pamphlets.' "

John Swithin chuckled. "Yes, you certainly are well informed."

"As I'm sure you are about me," added Eric, delighted to discover a lively companion in this country doctor.

"Well, how about ordering lunch now?" suggested Dr. Swithin, a gleam of satisfaction in his eyes.

It was over the second cup of rich, dark coffee that Dr. Swithin finally made his first move. He had it planned as if it were a game of chess, only in this instance he wanted his opponent's king to capture his queen. "I understand you met my daughter, Nicki, last summer when she was visiting the United States." He looked askance at Eric Damon, ready to note even the slightest change in pallor. But he met only disappointment as the other man answered coolly.

"Yes, your daughter and I met in New York."

So, that's how it's going to be, thought John Swithin. He's not exactly volunteering information. "Are you acquainted with my sister-in-law and her husband, the Bensons?"

"Yes, in fact, your daughter and I met at their apartment. I believe Maude and Bill were giving a cocktail party to introduce her to New York society." A wry smile flitted across his face.

"Oh, dear, I can imagine how my offspring must have loved that!"

"As a matter of fact, we met when I accidentally woke her up from a nap in Bill's study."

"Now that sounds like my Nicki," laughed her father.

"Yes, an interesting child," Eric replied in a noncommittal tone.

"She seemed to be quite impressed by you."

"Well, don't you think young girls are often impressed by an older man, especially one with a great deal of money?" His question was rhetorical, casual, but to the discriminating ear a certain brittleness could be detected.

"After all, I'm nearly sixteen years older than your daughter."

So, it's just possible, thought John Swithin, that I was right. Nicki may have walked all over this man's ego without even knowing it. He's trying to convince himself that she was just a schoolgirl with a crush on her first older man, her first older man with money, at that! "I suppose a man in your position has run into a few ambitious females."

"Don't kid yourself, Doctor, there is no such thing as a woman without ambition. I've never met one yet who didn't make the most of every opportunity thrown her way."

"You have a very cynical view of women, Mr. Damon. Perhaps you haven't met the right kind," John Swithin ventured.

"I have met every type; underneath they're all the same."

"That may be true for some women, but I can honestly tell you it isn't true for my daughter."

"There speaks a devoted father."

"Well, I don't suppose you got to know her that well in just two weeks."

"Two weeks?"

"Nicki was in New York just two weeks. She spent the rest of the summer in Maine."

"Yes, I know," Eric Damon said stiffly. "I think it's time we quit playing games with each other, Doctor Swithin. I have a summer home on Mount Desert Island. Nicki and I saw each other several times throughout the summer."

"Well, then you do know how unimportant money is to Nicki. Or for that matter the things that usually go with wealth—fame, power, social position. Besides, I suppose she may have told you . . ." He deliberately let his voice fade.

"Told me what?"

John Swithin knew he had the man's complete attention. "Oh, just that since she was seventeen or so, Nicki has had several offers from men in our district, asking her to marry them. Some were wealthy, although not in your league. One was older, nearer to my age than yours. She's even had a shot or two at a title."

"And?"

"And nothing. She turned them all down. Wasn't interested. But then you know what kind of girl Nicki is."

"What kind of girl she is?"

"Yes, I always knew that when Nicki married it would be for love and love alone. Not the kind that can be turned on and off like a faucet, but the steadfast kind of love that would always be with a man, warming him on the loneliest night whether she was there or not. When a man is loved like that, he knows he is loved for life!" And this time John Swithin knew he had discovered the chink in the man's armor, for Eric Damon's face grew dark with suppressed emotion.

"Dammit! All right, Doctor, I'll admit it, I couldn't figure Nicki out. A twenty-year-old kid had me stumped. I thought I knew it all when it came to women, but your daughter"—he shook his head—"for your daughter they should have written another chapter in the book."

"Some wise man once said it was easier to understand women than just one woman."

"He must have met your daughter."

"Nicki's just a simple country girl."

"Even you don't believe that. Oh, I'll admit she seemed genuine and open, without a deceptive bone in her body. I thought to myself—here's a sweet young girl with all of her dreams intact, yet she's woman enough to know who she is and what she wants out of life. A girl who deserves the best, even better than I could ever offer her." Eric broke off, running his hands through the gray-tinted hair at his temples. "She was only a figment of my imagination, it would seem."

Dr. Swithin let the man rattle on, recognizing the battle Eric Damon seemed to be fighting within himself.

"Is she happy?" Eric finally spoke again.

"Is she happy?"

"Yes, is Nicki happy?" And John Swithin could see by the gray pallor of his face what it had cost this proud man to ask that question.

"No—no, I'm afraid she's not."

Eric looked up sharply, studying the older man's face, his own a subtle study of the agony a man can feel. "She's not." His voice showed he had not considered that possibility. "Young Winstead isn't making her happy?"

"No, he's not."

"He's not! Why in the hell not?" His voice cracked slightly.

"Well, for one thing I don't suppose Mark's young bride would care for it much."

"Mark's bride?"

"Yes, he's only been married for a few days."

"Only a few days," Eric's voice seemed a long way off. "I-I don't understand."

"What don't you understand?" Dr. Swithin was deliberately being obtuse, but he had to be very sure of Eric Damon's feelings.

"I don't understand about Mark Winstead and Nicki. Isn't Nicki his bride?"

"Heavens, no," laughed the doctor. "They were old childhood friends, nothing more. Oh, for a while last

165

spring I thought it might develop into more, but it never really did, not on Nicki's part anyway. She wrote and told him so last summer while she was in America."

"You mean that Nicki is not married to Mark Winstead!" It was nearly an accusation.

"She's not married to anyone," her father said quietly.

"Oh—God," groaned the younger man; he turned his head away, averting his eyes from the other man's scrutiny. Minutes ticked by and still he did not speak.

"Are you all right, Eric?" John Swithin finally dared to ask. For a moment he wondered if he had carried his game too far. Yet he dared when the stakes were so high, he consoled himself.

"I thought—I thought Nicki was married to someone else all this time."

"Would that have mattered to you?"

"Yes. I don't mind telling you now, John, that I have been to hell and back these past three months!" But John Swithin could tell that he did mind making that kind of confession. Eric was not a man used to speaking of his feelings. "I may as well tell you I was in love with your daughter. I had made up my mind to ask Nicki to marry me—but we had a misunderstanding . . . or perhaps I was the one who misunderstood. Anyway, I had to go to New York to see my mother and unexpected circumstances kept me from returning to Maine at the time I had told Nicki I would be back. I thought she would be waiting for me, but when I did get back she was gone. I was told Nicki had flown home to be married." Eric's voice was low and harsh. "I couldn't even tolerate another human being around me for an entire month."

Neither man spoke for several minutes and when the silence was broken, it was by John Swithin. "If it makes any difference to you at all, Eric, I can tell you that Nicki has suffered too."

"What is she doing now?"

"Preparing for a career on the concert stage. She is supposed to join her godmother in Paris sometime in April."

"Is that what she really wants to do?"

"She *tells* me she wants to be a concert pianist."

"It just seems a little odd to me. My mother was a concert artist—I don't know if Nicki told you that?"

"No, she didn't."

"Nicki played for my mother in New York last summer, but when she asked Nicki if she was interested in pursuing a musical career your daughter answered that she wasn't equipped for that kind of life."

"People do change. They get tougher."

"And you think Nicki has changed?"

"She's grown up—she's lost her girlish innocent delight in the small pleasures of life. I did hate to see that go. It was a rare quality in a woman. Her spontaneous gift for laughter and fun has been replaced by a single-minded dedication to her career. Her natural openness has become elusive, her gaiety sobered. Yes, Nicki has changed."

The younger man by perhaps a dozen years stared straight into the grave face of the older man. "Do you believe that I've had something to do with the changes you see in your daughter?"

John Swithin looked up without uttering a word. He had reached the crossroads, the point of no return, and he knew it. What he chose to say now could determine his only child's future happiness. Would she thank her father for interfering in her life or would she resent his efforts? The responsibility he had assumed weighed heavily on Dr. Swithin's shoulders. Nicki had changed, that much was for certain. She was no longer the carefree girl who had eagerly dashed through the door of their bungalow late last spring to join her father for tea one more time before she left on her trip to America. But were the differences he saw simply a natural part of her maturing or was it this man across the table from him who was responsible for the wounded expression he had glimpsed in his daughter's eyes? Nicki had admitted that she was in love with Eric Damon. And if any doubts had existed in John Swithin's mind, they had been eradicated by the anguish he had heard in her voice as she spoke Eric's name. "Yes, I think you had something to do with it," he finally sighed.

A strange glint lit up the azure blue eyes of the waiting man. He suddenly looked younger; a hint of a smile touched his mouth. His companion was no less than amazed by the transformation.

"I realize that Nicki is your daughter and naturally, your first loyalties are with her. I also believe you want her happiness perhaps above all else. Believe me when I tell you that her happiness is of vital importance to me as well!" John Swithin patiently waited for Eric to make his point, but he asked a question of him instead. "Why did you ask me to meet you here today?"

The question caught Dr. Swithin off guard. It wasn't what he had expected next. There was only one answer he could give and that was the true one. "I wrote to you because my daughter is desperately unhappy and I think you're the reason."

Eric sat perfectly still. Then he released a long, drawn-out breath. "Look, Nicki and I were more than just friends this summer. I guess you've figured that out by now. For a while I even thought she might be falling in love with me. But she was so young and although there was no doubt that I was attracted to her, I just wasn't sure how deep my feelings did go. She wasn't like the other women in my life. She got under my skin, and to be honest with you I didn't like it, I fought it all the way. I had always thought there was no place in my life for marriage and all of a sudden I found myself thinking of marriage with a girl nearly half my age! I don't mind telling you that it scared the hell out of me. I went away for a few weeks and when I got back I had decided to ask Nicki to be my wife. But suddenly she was elusive, almost angry with me. She even told me she would never be interested in marrying a man like me. I wondered if I had somehow missed my chance with her. I decided to simply let nature take its course, with a little help from me. I hadn't counted on her leaving Bar Harbor while I was in New York. I thought she'd be waiting for me when I got back. When I found her gone, I thought that was simply the end of it, she hadn't loved me after all. I couldn't blame her for wanting someone her own age."

"Is that going to be the end now?"

"I don't know, I just don't know."

"Then I feel I must ask you a very personal question. Are you still in love with my daughter?"

Clear blue eyes held his for a moment before the answer was given. "Yes."

"Then you're a fool, man, if you've never told Nicki that!"

"I've never told her."

"Then the rest goes without saying."

"You don't pull any punches, do you, John?" But Eric was smiling broadly at the other man. "May I offer you a ride?"

"Where are you headed?"

"To a small village named Cheswick. I have some unfinished business with a young lady who lives there."

"No—I think I'll stay in London another night. I'm meeting some old friends for dinner at the club." He remained talking for several minutes with the younger man before they finally shook hands in parting. "Good luck, Damon. I'll give you one day to convince that daughter of mine and then I'll be home!"

"Yes, sir, I understand," chuckled Eric as he drove away.

CHAPTER NINE

Nicki had fixed herself a simple supper of eggs and tomatoes. She hadn't been very hungry anyway. Now it was eaten and her few dishes washed and put away and the long evening alone stretched out ahead of her. The television offered her no diversion and she felt too restless to curl up with a book as she often did in the evenings. She decided on an impulse to wash her hair rather than wait until morning. Gathering up shampoo and cream rinse, hair dryer and towel, she made her way back to the kitchen and dumped her armload of paraphernalia onto the counter by the sink. Then deciding that music would be a nice accompaniment to washing her hair, she padded down the hallway to the study, her raggedy blue bedroom slippers flapping with each step. Nicki picked out one of her favorite recordings and placed it on the stereo. Then she stood for a moment as the opening strains of Mozart's Symphony No. 40 in G minor filled the room. Turning the volume up as far as it would go, she sauntered back to the kitchen.

Dressed in faded jeans and an old shirt of her father's, she leaned over the sink and turned on the faucet. As soon as the water temperature was regulated she stuck her head under the warm water and proceeded to apply a generous portion of shampoo to her short wet curls. Humming under her breath, Nicki patted and swirled the soap bubbles through her hair, her foot tapping, hips swaying in time to the music. After two shampooings, Nicki rinsed out the soap and groped for the towel, wrapping it turban-style about her head. She turned off the faucet and patted her face dry.

The girl stopped dead in her tracks and sniffed—she smelled something burning. Was it smoke? Yes, it was tobacco smoke! Nicki swung around, her mouth falling open, for there was Eric Damon casually leaning against the kitchen doorway, a lit cheroot in his mouth. He was dressed in a dark blue casual suit with a lighter shade of shirt underneath that enhanced the color of his blue eyes, eyes that watched her with a general air of amusement.

"Eric!" The blood rushed to her face, her knees were suddenly weak with the emotions unleashed at the sight of him. Then terribly conscious of her old clothes, her shiny face without a speck of makeup, the towel wrapped around her wet head, she demanded angrily, "What are you doing here?" How could Eric be here now? Nicki was certain she had never looked worse, though in truth she was beautiful without any aids. How could Eric do this to her, she asked herself. Drat the man!

"What in the hell have you done to your hair?" Eric stepped forward and tore the towel from her head, his fingers touching the short wet curls beneath.

But the man's touch was tender. Nicki found herself trembling at his nearness—he still went to her head like

172

a potent brandy. She made herself pull away with a jerk. "I had it cut," she countered defensively.

"I can see that for myself, but whatever possessed you to have all that beautiful hair chopped off?"

"It wasn't 'chopped off'! I paid a small fortune to have it styled at a posh shop in Wolverhampton," she sniffed. "I'll have you know this is the latest hairdo."

"I liked it better the way you used to wear it."

"I felt like a change," she snapped back.

"I can see it hasn't improved your disposition any. Perhaps I should come back another time . . ."

"No, no, it's all right. I-I'm sorry, Eric," she said sheepishly. "You startled me appearing like that. A girl does hate to be caught looking less than her best." Recovering some of her natural poise she made him an offer. "I'll get you a drink and you give me ten minutes to change."

"All right."

"H-how did you get here anyway?" Nicki's breath caught in her throat.

"I drove down in my car," he answered in an offhand manner. It didn't tell the young woman what she wanted to know, but she vowed to ask him again just as soon as she changed out of these clothes into something presentable.

"The liquor cabinet is in the study. I don't even know what we have to offer you." Nicki left him there to his own devices, after modulating the sound of her stereo, and ran up the flight of stairs to her room. She pulled off the tattered jeans and shirt and darted under a hot shower. Toweling off, she slipped into lacy underthings and pulled a long flowing caftan over her head. By the time she tried to run a comb through the cluster of honey-colored curls, they were nearly dry. That would simply have to do, she thought as she stepped back to survey herself in the mirror, hazel eyes strangely bright and alive staring back at her. Not bad on such short notice, she reassured her image.

It was outside the door of the study that Nicki hesitated, suddenly a little frightened and shy at confronting the man who waited for her within. Earlier questions came back to haunt her. How did Eric get here? Why was he here? It was nearly three months since she had last seen him. Nicki was devastated to discover that his effect on her had not diminished. The sight of this tall muscular figure still set her emotions on a merry-go-round. Oh, God, why had Eric come back now? Was the bittersweet pain to begin all over again? She had worked so hard to convince herself that a career was her future, that she could find fulfillment in music. And now within moments this man had destroyed all of her illusions. She ached for him! Eric was her life, her only hope for the future.

But it didn't make sense to her—to just show up like this now. He must surely know that she wasn't married to Mark Winstead. Eric had come to the house as if he had known she would be there. How, that was the question? Well, you're never going to find out standing on this side of the door, she reproved herself.

"Your ten minutes are up!" Eric flung open the study door. "Oh—and here you are. How very punctual, my dear Nicki. But then punctuality is only one of your many assets." The implication was clear as his gaze raked up and down her body. Try as she may, Nicki could not prevent the soft pink flush from rising to her cheeks.

"Well, it is nice to know that some things in this life are constant—like your bad manners," she answered smoothly, slipping past him into the room. "I see you still delight in embarrassing me."

"It was meant as a compliment. The kind of compliment a man gives an attractive woman. But then she must be woman enough to recognize it as such," he replied sarcastically.

"I recognize *that* was no compliment," she answered coolly. Helping herself to a drink, she glided to the study window, her long dress gracefully brushing against her body. She stood there for a long moment gazing out at the night. Then the girl turned and spoke to Eric. "I assume you didn't come all this way to exchange insults with me, delightful though it may be."

"Sarcasm does not become a lovely lady, Nicki."

"Perhaps you don't bring out the 'lady' in me!"

"I'd be happy to just bring out the woman in you."

"You've always got an answer, don't you, Eric? Well, I give up. I can't compete with you anymore," she sighed, suddenly serious. A small white hand trembled as she reached up to brush away a stray curl.

"Men and women weren't meant to compete with each other, my love. They were meant to complement one another."

"No doubt another gem of wisdom garnered from your vast experience with women."

"Not nearly as vast as you imagine, my dear."

"Don't tell me you're an 'innocent'!"

"I didn't say that." Eric kept a firm grip on his temper. "A man in my position gets credited with numerous affairs he has never had. Surely you know enough about life to recognize that some women would do almost anything to get their name linked with mine. If I so much as show a simple common courtesy to a woman I read my name in the gossip columns the next day implying that another name has been added to my list. There isn't much a man can do to protect his name. When I was younger I thought it was amusing—now it's just a nuisance."

"And what of a woman like Nadine Cole? Don't tell me she's just a 'nuisance.' "

"I've never denied that at one time there was more between Nadine and me. But it was over long before I met you."

"How can you stand there and have the nerve to tell me that when I saw her with my own eyes in your apartment, with your pajamas on? Or half of them anyway!"

"Nicki, you must learn to trust me. I told you last summer not to jump to conclusions. There has been nothing between Nadine and me since I met you. I haven't been with anyone since that night we met in Bill's study." His voice was low but every word was audible. Nicki's heart was racing wildly as she considered his admission. "I haven't wanted anyone but you."

She fought back the memory of that morning in New York, of Nadine scantily clad in Eric's pajamas, but her confidence faltered. "Too bad Nadine didn't realize you no longer wanted her—or did you forget to tell her?"

"Don't be too hard on Nadine, little one, there's a lot about her that you don't know. I've never known you to be uncharitable."

"I'm sure you know her far better than I do." The sarcasm was plain.

"Look, Nicki, she's had a tough time since her husband died. I won't claim my motives were selfless, but she needed someone badly and I was a friend and I was there. Nadine was a beautiful woman, or at least I thought so until I got to really know her. That night after I left you I found Nadine on my doorstep, practically unconscious. It wasn't the first time either. My housekeeper put her to bed in the guest room as she had done before. It's a long story, so I'll just say that I discovered Nadine had a drinking problem after I had ended our brief relationship. She's an alcoholic, Nicki. Nadine is in a sanitorium now. I convinced her it was the only way when I was in New York last summer."

"Oh—" A frown formed on her face. "I-I've said some pretty terrible things, haven't I, Eric? Would it make any difference if I said I'm sorry?"

"It always makes a difference between us."

Suddenly a kernel of an idea took seed in Nicki's mind. "When you left Maine last summer to go see Louisa, did you see Nadine then too?"

"Yes."

"And you talked to her about going into the hospital?" She watched him nod his dark head. "And is that the reason you were late returning from New York?"

"Yes, it was."

"Oh, Eric, why didn't you call and tell me?" she cried out.

"Would it have made any difference? My dear child, would you have understood if I'd told you I was with Nadine? Would you have believed me if I'd tried to explain?"

"Perhaps not, but you didn't even give me the chance."

"You were so young, Nicki. I couldn't take that chance. As it was, I see now I should have told you everything."

"And Louisa—how is Louisa?"

"My mother is fine. I went straight to her apartment from the airport that day. We sat and chatted for a while as we usually did, she served sherry and cookies, and then I took her hand in mine and told her my story. She knew most of it, of course. But for the first time I heard about my father. It was a strange feeling. I was proud of her, Nicki. It hasn't been easy for her either. Louisa will be flying over to join me for Christmas. Perhaps you'll have a chance to come up to London to see her."

"Perhaps I will. I'd like to see her again."

"And me—would you like to see me again too?"

"I-I don't know." Nicki suddenly felt the need for something to do with her hands. She walked across the room to the makeshift bar and poured herself a glass of juice. Then the girl settled herself in a large, over-stuffed chair and lit up a cigarette.

"I didn't know you smoked," Eric commented, a curious expression on his handsome face.

"I didn't . . . that is, I-I usually don't."

"But you are now."

"Yes, I am now."

"Why? Do you smoke when you're nervous, on edge?"

"Sometimes."

"Are you nervous now, Nicki?"

"Why must you constantly badger me with questions? You're always at me!"

"I wasn't aware that I'm always at you, as you so prettily put it. I haven't laid a hand on you since I walked through that door!"

"Should I congratulate you on your self-control?"

"You're enough to infuriate the most patient of men."

"I didn't ask you to come here tonight, Eric. If you're finding it so difficult to be with me perhaps you should leave!"

"Perhaps I should!" There was dark fury etched on his features. Eric slammed his glass down on the nearest table and turned without a word and walked out of the room. Seconds later Nicki heard the front door shut behind him.

The young woman sat there for a moment before she realized her whole body was shaking. Damn him, damn the man! No, no it was her, she'd done it again. She'd let her temper get the best of her once more. She had driven him away and this time she knew in her heart that he

178

would not come back. Well, when you do something, you do it up big, my dear girl. No halfway measures for you. Your silly pride got in the way again and you've just sent away the only man you'll ever love. Oh, you've kept your precious pride all right, but what good will it do you now? What is pride worth without the man you love at your side? It isn't any comfort, is it, Nicki? Then for God's sake, woman, go after him before it is too late!

"Eric!" Nicki jumped up from her chair and ran to open the study door. "Eric, I'm . . ." She stuttered to a stop and stood there in the hallway staring at the dark outline of a man leaning against the front door, her face ravaged by the love she felt for him. "Eric?" Her voice was small; she wasn't certain she had even said his name aloud.

"I couldn't leave, Nicki. I couldn't leave like that knowing I'd never see you again." She saw her own pain reflected in his face, her own torment in his eyes. "I just couldn't walk away as if it didn't matter."

"A-and I couldn't let you go." Her hand lifted in a tentative gesture of appeal. "Come back in, Eric. Let's start over, as if you'd just arrived. All right?"

"All right." He slowly straightened up to his full height and walked back toward her. Nicki turned and went into the study, trusting him to follow her.

"Are you in London for long?" She felt as though she was making inane conversation, but she knew she must say something to heal the breach between them, to keep him here beside her.

"I'm doing some consultant work for the next few weeks and then after the holidays I may go to France for a vacation. I've been working night and day for the past three months."

"Is everything all right?"

"No, no it's not."

"I'm sorry, I imagine a man in your position has a lot of worries."

"That's true." Eric grew strangely quiet, as if he were brooding over something.

"But surely you have any number of assistants who can help you."

"No—some problems a man must work out for himself." Then he turned to face the young woman standing across the room from him. "Why didn't you tell me you weren't married to Mark Winstead?"

Nicki was momentarily taken aback by his question. She looked up at him almost as if she hadn't heard him correctly.

"Why didn't you let me know, Nicki?"

"I guess I thought it wouldn't interest you."

"You thought it wouldn't interest me!"

"We haven't exactly kept in touch."

"I would always love keeping in touch with you." There was a funny little smile on his face.

Nicki ignored this last remark of Eric's. "I-I haven't known very long about the mix-up, about what Clare told you, that is. Her letter just arrived a few days ago. She had forgotten to tell me. I didn't know until then," she added softly.

"Why didn't you tell me last summer that you'd written to Mark calling it all off between the two of you?"

"I don't know, Eric. Perhaps I was afraid you would see it as a ploy, a move to pressure you into something you weren't sure of. But, how did you know I'd written Mark? I haven't told anyone but my father."

"I had lunch with your father today, Nicki."

"You what?"

"Your father and I lunched together just a few hours ago."

180

"But how? Why?"

"I received a letter from him last week asking me to meet him in London at my convenience."

"But why would he do a thing like that?" The girl's face was flushed with confusion.

"He seemed to think that you were unhappy—and that I was the reason."

"Did he tell you that?"

"Yes."

"He had no right, no right at all to say that to you!" she cried out, her cheeks red with humiliation, her back straight as a poker.

"He only wanted your happiness."

"I don't care. He had no business to go behind my back, to humiliate me like that. Well, it does explain one thing to me. I know why you're here. You can take your pity and go to the devil, Eric Damon!"

"Now wait a minute, Nicki—"

"Oh, you're absolutely oozing with magnanimity, aren't you? No wonder you look so self-satisfied, gloating over another apparent easy victory!"

"Well, is it true, Nicki?"

"Is what true?" she ground through her teeth.

"Are you still in love with me?"

"I wouldn't give you the satisfaction of knowing the answer to that question," she snarled at him. "I-I think I hate you!"

"I don't believe you hate me, but you force me to find out for myself," he said menacingly as he moved toward her.

"Keep away from me," Nicki whispered desperately.

"Why? You've nothing to fear if you hate me as much as you claim." Eric reached out his hand to touch her arm.

"It would seem you don't have much on under the gown you're wearing." His voice was low and seductive.

"You'll never have the opportunity to find out," she spat at the man as she turned and made a dash for the study door.

"Nicki—Nicki, why do you fight me so?" Laughing low, Eric caught her about the waist as she tried to escape and pulled her to him. Nicki twisted and turned in his arms, trying to break his hold on her. She finally resorted to physical violence, kicking him as hard as she could in the shin. Eric, caught unaware, doubled over in pain and in that moment Nicki pushed herself away from him. But the man's reflexes were quicker; he lunged for the girl and they landed, the man's weight crushing her beneath him, on the edge of the sofa.

"There's only one way to tame a wildcat!" Eric growled as his mouth came down on hers, grinding Nicki's teeth into her lips. The assault on her senses was relentless, without mercy, as if the man were determined to punish her for the pain he had suffered, was still suffering if the truth were known. Nicki struggled against him as a frightened, wild creature will fight its captor until it reaches the point of exhausted capitulation. Her lips were numb from his bruising kisses, her body breathless as his weight bore her down into the cushions.

Then, as if his anger were finally assuaged, Eric's embrace became tender, his kiss gentle, as he softly molded her mouth to his own. His hands began to caress rather than wound her. He sought to teach the girl to trust him, to lead the way for both of them. Nicki ceased her struggling and simply lay in his arms trying to decide if she could trust this apparent change in his attitude. Then she finally expelled a long sigh and stopped fighting him. Wrapping her arms about his waist, she pressed him even

182

closer to her own pliable form. Nicki returned kiss for kiss, her own longing, her own growing excitement matching Eric's at every step.

Eric's kiss became longer, deeper, more demanding as he wrung the very soul from Nicki's body. He was asking everything of her and she was no longer afraid to give all she had, no longer afraid to lose herself in the passions he aroused in her.

"Oh, Eric," she moaned. "Please—I want you so!"

"No—no, listen, Nicki, we've got to talk while we still can," he mumbled in a thick voice, suddenly aware of just how close they had come to the point of not turning back.

"No, I don't want to talk now," she pouted. "I want to kiss you. I never want to stop." And with that Nicki reached up and pulled Eric's dark head down to hers.

"Nic . . ." he started to protest, but her sweet lips were a sore temptation to the man, a temptation that he could not resist. Her mouth opened gladly to his as they drowned together in a sea of sensuous emotions. Nicki took his strong brown hand in hers and raised it to her lips, kissing the palm before she placed it over her heart.

With a supernatural effort, Eric pushed himself away from the lovely creature beneath him and sat up, trembling visibly as he sought deep within himself for some measure of self-control. The girl gazed up at him with soft eyes full of his lovemaking. "Look here, Nicole Swithin, you sit up in that corner over there and behave yourself! I came here tonight to say something to you and by God, I'm going to get it said if it's the last thing I do!"

"I-I only want you, Eric," she whispered.

"Well, I want more!" he blurted out, startling the pale young woman who sat only inches away. "Don't you understand what I'm trying to say to you?" And he watched as she shook her head no. "You're not making this any easier for me, Nicki."

"Not making what any easier for you? Eric, I just don't understand what you want me to say."

"If there was ever a time in your life to be totally honest with yourself and with me, that time is now, my darling. Nicki—are you in love with me?"

Nicole Swithin gazed up into the man's face that was so near to her own. He seemed older somehow, or was it that he looked terribly tired? Yes, Eric looked as though he had been on a long journey. And there was something more to be read there if only she dared to believe it. Was it desperation she saw in his eyes? Could it possibly be that he was afraid to hear her answer because it might be no? But it wasn't, of course, and she took a deep breath before she spoke. "Yes, Eric, I'm in love with you still."

"Oh, my darling girl," he said gathering her to him. "Will you marry me, Nicki? Will you be my wife?"

Nicki squeezed her eyes tightly shut. She had never thought to hear those words from Eric, she had never imagined her dreams would be within her grasp. But he had not said the words she must hear from his lips. "I-isn't this a bit sudden?" she murmured against his chest. A fearful suspicion grew in her mind. "I mean, you made no attempt to see me for over three months and then my father writes to you, you meet for lunch, and presto, the next thing I know you're proposing to me. I can't believe my dear father would or even could blackmail you—I just don't understand how he got you to agree to marry me, or why."

"Dammit, woman, your father had nothing to do with this—well, only that without his well-intentioned interference I would never have known that you weren't married to another man! Do you have any idea what it did to me believing that some other man had the right to claim your kisses for his own, that he was making love to your sweet young mind and body? I was so sore at you after you walked out on me last summer that I wasn't fit company for another human being for weeks. God, Nicki, don't you know the hell you've put me through? Can't you see that I'm hopelessly, desperately, out of my mind with love for you?"

The young woman sat staring at the handsome man beside her, afraid to believe what her ears had heard.

"Well, don't you have anything to say?"

"Y-you love me?" her voice cracked.

"Yes, I love you, Nicki. I came here tonight to tell you that and to ask you to marry me."

"You want to marry me?" she echoed.

"Yes—haven't you heard a word I've said? I want you, Nicki. I want you to be my wife, the mother of the children I never thought I'd be lucky enough to have! Now close your eyes for a moment, I have a surprise for you." As he spoke Eric drew a small velvet jeweler's box from his pocket. "This is something I should have done a long time ago. I was a fool, I let you slip through my fingers." Before the girl knew what had happened Eric had slipped a cold metal ring onto her hand. "You can open your eyes now," he prompted her.

But the young woman sat there, frozen to the spot, afraid to open her eyes and seize the opportunity for happiness offered to her. Happiness had seemed such a tenuous commodity to her over the past few months. She dared not open her eyes and break the spell—it was all a dream that would fade away, she told herself. She would awaken any moment now and find herself alone once more.

"For God's sake, Nicki, open your eyes and say something—anything!" he pleaded with her. Then Eric stood up abruptly and looked down at the girl, but he could stand the suspense no longer. He went over to the bar and poured himself a generous portion of brandy, which he swallowed in one single gulp. Then he poured himself another drink and stood there with his back to her, the glass in his hand.

Nicki slowly opened her hazel eyes and stared into the glowing heart of the large yellow diamond on her finger. Her heart was pounding wildly. It was the most beautiful ring she had ever seen in her life, and Eric had given it to her! He did love her, after all. It was almost more than she could bear.

"Is—is it because you don't love me enough?" he finally asked with his back still to her. "I know a woman can love a man but not want to marry him. I've seen that too many times in my circle of acquaintances. Or is it because of the other women in my past? Because if it is I promise you will be the only one in my future, the only woman for the rest of my life. Unless it's because you feel I'm too old for you? I'm afraid I can't change that much as I wish I could. God, I wish I were ten years younger! I've loved you for a long time, Nicki, even though I may never have told you so. I've loved you longer than you'll ever know."

"H-how long?" she finally asked.

"I bought that ring in New York last summer. I've carried it around with me ever since, but I couldn't tell you why. That night we met on the beach at Bar Harbor was no accident. I knew you were there with your . . . your friend. I was going to give you the ring that night, I was going to ask you to marry me then."

"Why didn't you?" she cried out.

"I foolishly thought if you really cared about me you would let me make love to you. When you pulled back at the last moment I wasn't sure how you felt. But I realized you might need more time and that you were different from the other women I had known. So I was planning to ask you just as soon as I got back from New York. Things didn't work out as I had planned—you were gone." The pain in his voice was evident.

"I didn't know, Eric," she said softly.

"I guess I won't be needing this after all," he muttered sardonically as he took a slim white envelope from his suit pocket.

"What is it?" Nicki held her breath.

"A special marriage license."

"Eric Damon! I wouldn't have believed that a man like you would give up so easily!" she said sharply. He turned to face her, an inscrutable expression on his handsome features. "You haven't even given me a chance to answer your first question. You've been rattling on and on as though you thought I didn't love you. Don't you know that I would follow you to hell and back! Because I would, you know. I've had a bad time the past few months, too. How do you think I felt believing that the only man I would ever love, that the only man I would ever want to marry, didn't believe in marriage, had never told me that he loved me? Oh, Eric, how could you?" Her eyes swelled with tears, but before they had reached her cheeks, he was there beside her, holding her as though he would never let her go.

"We've been a fine pair of fools, my dear," Eric whispered against her lips. "Thank God your father came to me. I won't even let myself think what would have happened if he hadn't. To spend the rest of my life without you . . . I couldn't have done it, my love."

"I'm still going to have a talk with him," laughed Nicki.

"Listen, my girl, he didn't give away any of your secrets until I'd told him exactly how I felt about you. His strategy was flawless. Your father is no one's fool. I liked him."

"I can't wait to tell him how well he succeeded at playing Cupid."

"We're to meet your father and the vicar at the chapel at ten o'clock sharp tomorrow morning."

"Well!"

"He simply had confidence in me, my love. I think he suspected that one way or another it would work out for the best. I hope you'll forgive me for choosing your wedding dress for you. It's in the car along with some other things. Your father has agreed to drive us to the airport and tomorrow afternoon our plane leaves for Greece. A friend has loaned us his villa—a lovely and very secluded house by the sea. In a few short hours, my darling Nicki, you will be Mrs. Eric Damon!"

"Eric!"

"What is it, Nicki? Am I going too fast for you? You haven't really said that you'll marry me, have you? I can't wait any longer for you, Nicki. I want you now!"

"And I want you! But what about your conferences . . . your work?"

"They'll have to get someone else. What about the concert career?"

"I love you, Eric. I want to be your wife."

"I'm a crusty bachelor, my love, and we have been known to cross swords before."

"We always seem to start out fighting and end up making love." She curled her arms tight around him.

"That's the way it is sometimes between a man and a woman. It makes the loving that much sweeter, my pet."

"Will it always be that way between us, Eric?"

"Always."

"Don't let me go!"

"Never from this moment on, darling," and Eric's lips once more claimed hers with a promise for the future.